Scandal at the Palace

Royal romances fit for the headlines!

Five years after the death of his wife, reclusive King Jozef is stepping out of the shadows back into the royal spotlight. For the sake of his grown-up sons, Axel and Liam, he'll show his citizens he's still alive and well, and even go on a date or two...

A secret fling with the PR woman sent to help him is *not* part of the plan...but totally irresistible!

Read King Jozef and Rowan's story in

His Majesty's Forbidden Fling

Meanwhile, Princes Axel and Liam are embroiled in their own royal scandals.

Don't miss their stories, coming soon!

Dear Reader,

His Majesty's Forbidden Fling takes us to Prosperita, a thriving island in the Mediterranean. King Jozef Sokel lost his wife five years ago, and with his sons suddenly grown up, he finds himself alone. Or at least as alone as a person can be when every moment of his life is orchestrated by his schedule and watched by the media.

Enter Rowan Gray, the PR person hired to help repair his image. Not only is she courageous enough to stand up to him, but she's also beautiful and smart. He's smitten before he has a chance to keep himself from falling. But she's younger than he is and a career woman. He couldn't possibly drag her into the life he's forced to live.

Still, he can't keep his eyes or his mind off her and they begin a secret affair. But when longing turns to real love, he can't deny reality. They cannot be together except in the shadows.

It was extremely fun for me to write Jozef and Rowan's story, especially with Prosperita's two handsome princes waiting in the wings to find their own Cinderellas.

Happy reading!

Susan Meier

His Majesty's Forbidden Fling

Susan Meier

Recycling programs for this product may not exist in your area.

ISBN-13: 978-1-335-73672-7

His Majesty's Forbidden Fling

For questions and comments about the quality of this book, please contact us at CustomerService@Harlequin.com.

Harlequin Enterprises ULC
22 Adelaide St. West, 41st Floor
Toronto, Ontario M5H 4E3, Canada
www.Harlequin.com

Printed in U.S.A.

Susan Meier is the author of over fifty books for Harlequin. *The Tycoon's Secret Daughter* was a Romance Writers of America RITA® Award finalist, and *Nanny for the Millionaire's Twins* won the Book Buyers Best Award and was a finalist in the National Readers' Choice Awards. Susan is married and has three children. One of eleven children herself, she loves to write about the complexity of families and totally believes in the power of love.

Books by Susan Meier

Harlequin Romance

A Billion-Dollar Family

Tuscan Summer with the Billionaire
The Billionaire's Island Reunion
The Single Dad's Italian Invitation

Christmas at the Harrington Park Hotel

Stolen Kiss with Her Billionaire Boss

The Missing Manhattan Heirs

Cinderella's Billion-Dollar Christmas
The Bodyguard and the Heiress
Hired by the Unexpected Billionaire

Reunited Under the Mistletoe

Visit the Author Profile page
at Harlequin.com for more titles.

Praise for Susan Meier

"The perfect choice. I read this in one sitting; once I started, I couldn't put it down. *The Bodyguard and the Heiress* will put a smile in your heart. What I love most about Susan Meier's books is the joy your heart feels as you take the journey with characters that come to life. Love this book."

—*Goodreads*

CHAPTER ONE

KING JOZEF SOKOL settled himself in his seat in the private box at the Royal Theater of Prosperita. He did not want to be there, but his sons had arranged for him to join them for the opera and it was non-negotiable. They'd been hounding him for weeks about the fact that he was rarely seen in public anymore. Though he hated buckling under, he'd seen the true concern on their faces, and he'd decided to give in.

Once.

Just this once. There was nothing wrong with his life. Liam and Axel were simply being overly protective.

He smiled at the royal photographer and nodded to let him know he was dismissed after only one whirr of the camera. This wasn't a photo shoot. It wasn't even an opportunity for the press. It was as close as he would come to alleviating the fears of his sons that something serious was wrong with him. Particularly since they were overreacting, assuming he was depressed or worse, because he hadn't appeared in public in weeks…

Well, months—closer to a year, actually. But he didn't quibble over little things like that. He enjoyed his privacy. He enjoyed his work as ruler of a small, thriving island. His days had become a routine that guaranteed Prosperita stayed number one in the Mediterranean in terms of agricultural goods and the manufacturing and export of specialty equipment.

He sat up straighter, trying to get comfortable. He knew people in the theater's audience could turn and see glimpses of him, even with the box's lights down. Which was fine. His subjects were respectful and wouldn't react, beyond nudging their companions and discreetly pointing out that he was at the royal theater, out and about. If enough people noticed, he wouldn't have to do this again for another year or so.

He leaned into the velvet Queen Anne chair—uncomfortable things for a box designed for royalty—and made a mental note to have these chairs changed. A program sat on a silver tray atop the elbow-height table to his right. He opened it and scanned the names of the performers.

The sound of the curtain behind him sliding

open rolled into the royal box. Assuming his sons were arriving, he turned and saw a tall woman with long, curly auburn hair. Dressed in a purple strapless gown that showed off milky white shoulders and a long length of shapely leg where the dress was split up the side, she walked directly to the chair beside his and sat.

His chest tightened and something weird happened to his breathing. And not because of fear—which is what his reaction should have been, given that a stranger had infiltrated the most exclusive area in the theater. His breathing had stuttered because the woman was stunning.

He shook his head to clear it. Her intrusion into the royal box without permission was against the law. Pressing the discreet button for security, he glared at her. "Who are you?"

She offered her hand to shake his. "Rowan Gray."

She said it as if he should have known her. Then he wondered where the hell his security detail was. Not because they hadn't scrambled in at his beck and call, but because she'd gotten in at all. He hadn't heard anyone talking, asking to be granted entry.

Security had let her in without as much as a question?

"How did you get in here?"

"I have ways."

His jaw dropped. "Don't be flip! This is the *royal* box. You don't get in here without an engraved invitation."

She handed him a business card. He glanced down and saw it belonged to one of his sons.

"That's engraved. It's just not an invitation." She shrugged. "But I'll remember that for next time."

She handed him another card. This one had her name on it.

He met her gaze. "Sterling, Grant, Paris?"

"Your PR firm."

He groaned. What the hell were his kids up to? Yes, they had concerns about him not getting out in public much. But this was ridiculous. "Seriously?"

"It's why the guards didn't stop me. They were informed I'd be here."

He blew his breath out on a long sigh. He would dispatch her in short order and then find his sons. "I didn't authorize you."

"Castle Admin did."

That stopped him. Castle Administration was the name used for the staff for the royals. Typically, they followed his orders. But there were times they could make decisions about things that fell under their purview. The choice of dinnerware for a state dinner. Whom to invite to a royal ball. Authorization of trips to other countries or for visits to their country. And anything they believed was necessary for the betterment of Prosperita, which sometimes gave them latitude he didn't like. This wasn't merely a family matter anymore. It had grown into something he might not be able to control.

"My sons went over my head?"

She shrugged those perfect white shoulders. "Ech. What does it matter?"

He turned to one of his guards who had finally arrived. "Tomorrow morning, I want Joaquim in my office. I have serious concerns about our security."

"Yes, Your Majesty."

He handed Rowan's two cards to her. "You're fired."

She settled into the chair. "No. Theoretically, you didn't hire me so you can't fire me. Plus, we have work to do. I'm thrilled that you decided to come out in public for this performance—"

"For my sons."

She inclined her head, causing her pretty curls to shuffle. "It's a good start, but you need to say something to the press when you leave. Just say, 'the opera was lovely,' while you're racing down the stairs before your security team escorts you into your private elevator that will take you to your limo in the parking facility on the ground floor."

"No."

Her delicate eyebrows rose. "No?"

He didn't want to make a scene by standing and pointing at the curtain and ordering her to leave. God knew how many camera lenses from cell phones were pointed at him right now.

He tried the easy way, smiling and saying, "I didn't hire you. I don't want you. I don't need you. I'm not going to do what you say."

She laughed.

Her impertinence infuriated him, but he suddenly noticed that her shiny auburn hair cascaded down her naked back. The color set off her creamy skin, so smooth and white that it probably never saw the sun. It also accented her green eyes.

He blinked, taken aback by the fact that he even noticed her looks. Worse, his heart rate had accelerated, and his pulse had scrambled.

He'd been married for over two decades before his wife passed five years ago, and he'd never felt this overwhelming desire to stare at a woman. He'd never been sucked in by a woman's beauty. And he wouldn't be now. If his sons or the castle staff thought it was funny to throw a beautiful woman at him to see if he turned into a wimp who would melt at her feet and do what she wanted, they were crazy.

He was a king.

Kings did not melt.

They did what the hell they wanted.

He rose from his seat and walked out of the box, jogging down the stairs with his security detail scrambling after him. Ten steps on the edge of the almost empty lobby took him to a private elevator. He got in and rode to the ground floor, where a tunnel took him to parking accommodations for his limo.

He hated that *she* knew that.

He collapsed onto the back seat, wondering what in the hell had happened to his world—

He shook his head. What was to wonder about? He was a forty-five-year-old father whose children had come of age. That's what had happened. Liam was twenty-five and Axel was twenty-three.

It appeared they didn't like how he chose to live, and they had taken matters into their own hands. Two pups who didn't know a damned thing about real life were nosing into his?

That he would deal with swiftly.

Rowan watched him go with a heavy sigh, but she also had to admit she needed a moment—maybe the rest of the night—to regroup before she saw him again.

First, he was a king, and he wasn't pleased

that his sons had done an end run around him and hired a PR firm. He could be her most difficult client ever.

Second, no one had told her this guy was smoking hot and had the kind of accent that could melt butter. His Mediterranean island had been under British rule for a century before it gained independence. The residents didn't merely speak English. Their dialect combined the lovely melodious tones of their natural voices with British pronunciations.

Plus, forty-five wasn't old, and his glorious head of black hair made him look thirty-five. Muscles that moved beneath his jacket showed he obviously worked out. Add a black tux with a royal sash across his chest that had real medals and he was…

Tempting. Enticing. Intoxicating.

Those words never crossed her mind with clients. Never.

But holy everything, the man dripped sex appeal.

Needing to get home to her computer to investigate a few things before she reported back to her boss, she left the opera as inconspicuously as she had arrived, which was one of the fun things about being in PR. One minute she would be rubbing elbows with the rich and famous and the next she was walking in a warm July night to her rented sport utility vehicle. No security. No one noticing.

Though if anyone knew she'd just been with King Jozef, they'd be hounding *her* for a comment. The man hadn't spoken to the press in a year and he was handing out jobs to his sons like a monarch looking to retire, and despite how gorgeous he was, there was something brooding and haunted in his dark eyes.

Which unfortunately made him all the sexier.

She jumped in her car, admitting to herself that she didn't understand his recent withdrawal from the world. His wife had been gone for five years and from everything she'd read to prepare for this assignment, he and his queen had had a great marriage. He should have positive feelings about love and relationships and be eager to find someone.

She unexpectedly envied him. After the way her fiancé publicly humiliated her, she'd thrown herself into her work and was happy to be a successful woman who didn't need a man in her life, but some days—

She shook her head at the tiny spark of loneliness that formed in her chest. Because it was tiny. Barely discernible. And probably caused by the tingly feelings that had arisen around the handsome King. She didn't want them. Didn't trust them. She'd been the most naively trusting woman in the world until her fiancé had pulled the rug out from under her by running away with her best friend and getting married a week before *their* wedding.

Who in their right mind would even consider trusting again after publicly being made a fool?

Not her. She would never risk that kind of pain again. She had absolutely no idea how a heart expanded enough to love again, but she did know King Jozef shouldn't have the kinds of reservations she did. He was handsome, sought after, and had a stellar relationship in his past. The kind of relationship that should make him want another—

So why was he hiding? Why did he seem to prefer to be alone?

Her brain back in work mode, she called a few of her media sources in Prosperita as she drove to the small apartment Sterling, Grant, Paris had rented for her stay. She breathed a sigh of relief, when none of them knew anything about the King even having been at the theater, let alone leaving abruptly.

Maybe she'd get lucky, and no one would have noticed Jozef racing out before the opera even started.

She winced. Doubtful. Somebody always saw something. Like it or not, *she'd* been the one who caused him to do the one thing that would make his refusal to appear in public even shakier: run out like his feet were on fire.

She would check what the papers printed *before* they hit the stands and then she'd talk to her boss.

Jozef climbed the grand stairway of the silent foyer. He should have taken an elevator, but something drew him to the elegant winding stairway in the dark, quiet castle. He wasn't expecting to run into either of his sons. Most likely they were hiding. But first thing in the morning, they would be getting a sermon they would never forget. They wouldn't interfere in his life again.

The echoing expanse of the castle pressed in on him, as his quiet footfalls took him to the door at the back of the long second-floor hall that led to his quarters. He knew why the place felt so empty. He was alone. Wife gone. Children grown.

Stepping into the foyer of his apartment, he shook his head and told himself to stop being silly. So it was quiet? So he was alone?

He was a king with responsibilities, two sons, tons of friends. Hell, he was friends with the people who ruled the world. No. He *was* one of the people who ruled the world. He had nothing to be moody about.

He walked through his formal living room, the library and his home office to his bedroom suite. The second he stepped inside and saw his wife's picture on the bedside table, he knew why he was moody. He'd met a pretty woman that night and he'd reacted like a randy teenager. His breathing had all but stopped, his pulse had raced. It was a miracle he hadn't stuttered.

He sat on the bed and lifted his wife's portrait. No one wore a crown like Annalise had. She might not have been breathtaking like Rowan Gray, but she had been beautiful. She'd lit royal events. She'd made Christmas with their sons personal. She done her job with dignity and poise. Even after she'd gotten sick.

And he'd let his head be turned by somebody who was closer to his son's age than his own.

He returned the picture to its spot, telling himself he'd succumbed to biology—a racing heart and weird breathing were nothing but physiology—and went to bed.

His big, empty bed in his silent, silent world.

Up until tonight the quiet had been his sanctuary. Now suddenly it felt like a prison.

CHAPTER TWO

THE NEXT MORNING, his phone woke him with pings for texts from his sons, who apologized because they wouldn't be at breakfast, and a text from Castle Admin that read very much like a reprimand. An astute reporter had noticed Jozef's escape the night before, and their news outlet was reporting that something had to have been wrong with the King, given the expression on his face and the way he ran out.

He rolled his eyes. First his sons, then Castle Admin and now the press were homed in on him, as if he were crazy.

Oh, he definitely would handle this today.

He dressed in black trousers and a white oxford cloth shirt and headed downstairs.

Two members of Castle Admin—Art Andino, a tall, thin man in wire frame glasses, and Mrs. Jones, an older woman who had served as his mother's assistant for decades and now was head of "continuity"—stood just outside the door to the informal dining room and followed him to the table. They stopped beside two seats on the left.

An unfamiliar man in a gray suit sat at the far end of the table. And *she* was sitting at the chair right beside *his*.

Her glorious red-brown hair had been wound into a clumsy knot at the top of her head that allowed strands to escape and frame her face. She wore a unisex black suit with a white shirt open at the throat that somehow made her all the more feminine.

His heart jumped. All his nerve endings jingled.

He straightened his shoulders and took the power afforded him as ruler. Continuing the walk to his seat, he said, "Good morning, everyone."

Castle Admin said, "Good morning, Your Majesty."

The man in the gray suit and pretty Rowan gave him the courtesy demanded by his office and rose as they said, "Good morning, Your Majesty."

Before he got to his seat, he addressed her directly. "Why are you here? I fired you last night."

"Yes, you did, Your Majesty. But because you didn't hire me you can't fire me." She pointed at the man in the gray suit. "That's Peter Sterling, my boss."

"Perhaps I can fire him?"

Peter looked ready to faint or hyperventilate. Jozef knew he was imposing. Tall. Sturdy. With eyes that warned an adversary not to cross him.

Still, Pete said, "Actually, Your Majesty, Castle Admin hired me."

"Then maybe I should fire them?"

Mrs. Jones's eyes grew huge with fear. Stuffy Art Andino shifted from one foot to the other. Tension hung in the air.

Jozef took his seat, allowing everyone to take theirs. "And why are you here, Mrs. Jones?"

She shot him a sly look. "Moral support?"

He had to stifle a laugh. He'd known Ella Jones his entire life. If she felt he needed moral support, then shivering in their boots or not, they really were ganging up on him.

And something really was wrong.

Rowan said, "Somebody got a picture of you racing out of the theater last night and sold it to everyone. This morning's articles in all the news outlets are similar, reporting that you appear to be ill. You're thin and pale. Tired looking."

"I see." Though he wasn't pleased with the casual way she spoke to him, he suddenly understood the fuss. In the months before his wife's illness had been officially announced, she'd lost weight and had withdrawn. No wonder his subjects were sensitive to his isolation. They worried he was going down the same path his wife had, waiting until she was terminal to announce her illness.

Rowan gave him a quick once-over, the purely clinical assessment of a PR person. "Honestly, the comments baffle me. You look great to me—really great—for a guy of your age."

He balked. "I'm forty-five, not eighty-five." Still, her compliment went through him like a bolt of sexual electricity.

And finally, the reaction struck the right chord. There was no denying that he had a real, honest-to-God attraction to this woman who wanted to work for him. But in a way that was good. Knowing that what he was feeling wasn't fleeting, admitting it was real, he knew how to dismiss it.

Her boss shifted on his seat. "This doesn't have to be a big deal. The way I see it, you simply need to get out a few times in the next two months, so your subjects can see you're happy and healthy and stop the questions."

"The questions?" He turned his gaze on Mrs. Jones.

Her face flushed. "People have been questioning your sons for weeks. Every time you send one of them to an event you usually attend, the organizers and participants seek them out, ask if you're okay."

He took a long, resigned breath. He'd made the correct guess about why this was getting blown out of proportion. But that meant he had to address his subjects' concerns. Whether he needed a PR firm to do it was still up in the air.

The server arrived with Jozef's breakfast and Peter Sterling started talking again. "Your Majesty," he said, his voice dripping with respect for Jozef's position. "We believe all you need to do is go to some fundraisers. Perhaps a soccer game."

But Rowan eyed him, as if appraising him for sale at an auction. "I don't think fundraisers and soccer games are going to do it. I think he needs to go on a few dates."

Dates?

Gobsmacked into silence, Jozef only stared at her.

Rowan continued talking about him as if he were an inanimate object who couldn't hear or speak for himself. "Two dates. With two different women, spaced properly so no one thinks he has a new love interest, but also it won't appear he's gone off the deep end by dating so many different women he looks sleazy. We need to make him look like a normal guy, with normal…feelings."

Her candor rendered him speechless. But just when he was about to tell her to watch her step with him, everything she said fell into place in his brain, and he saw her point. His subjects deserved to have their fears relieved. More than that, though, given his abrupt and strong reaction to Rowen, he wondered if his body wasn't telling him something. Oh, he didn't want to get married again, or even settle in with one woman. But forty-five wasn't old enough to put himself out to pasture. A date every once in a while wasn't out of line.

He said, "Okay." But he wasn't letting a stranger choose his dates. He would pick the women he spent time with. "I will find two women and go out on two dates in the next four weeks."

He was about to dismiss them when the waitstaff returned with breakfast for Rowan and her boss. Mrs. Jones and Art Andino discreetly left, apparently already having eaten, but also satisfied that he'd agreed to go out in public again.

As the waitstaff left, Pete said, "It's not a good idea for you to choose your own dates." He winced. "I'm sorry if I sound disrespectful, but these first two dates—maybe even three—need to be chosen with care. You need to be seen with the right women who will project the correct image."

Annoyed that Pete hadn't simply taken him at his word the way Castle Admin had, he smiled his most kingly smile and said, "I thank you for your opinion. But I can handle this. In fact, rather than date, I can more easily clear everything up in one press conference. I won't mince words." He never did. "I'll apologize for isolating myself and I'll assure them I'm fine."

Sterling grimaced and carefully said, "I'm sorry again, but that won't work."

Rowan said, "If you hold a press conference to tell people you're fine, you'll look like you're making excuses. A guy who is fine is out in the world, doing his job and socializing. You haven't been. A slow, steady campaign of getting you out in public again would work best. You're also going to have to take back a few of the royal appearances you gave to your sons and you're going to have to be social. Not just rubbing elbows at state dinners. But dating. So we can avoid more articles like these—"

She pointed at the newspapers strewn across the table.

King races from theater.
Pale and drawn, King not strong enough to stay for entire performance.
What's the castle hiding?

Josef frowned. He never let his subjects worry or allowed the press to whip them into a frenzy. How had he missed that suspicion was growing or that the press was fanning the fires?

Pete rose. "Plus, you're in great hands. Rowan is old enough to have sufficient experience with the PR end of things and young enough that she's still in touch with trends etc. She knows to find you someone more like Adele than Lady Gaga."

Josef shifted his gaze to Rowan and she smiled at him.

"She'll also choose your wardrobe and write quick, snappy lines you can shoot at the press if they ask you questions... And you want them to. You want to get your message out to the public."

Holding her gaze, he realized again how young she was, and knew there could be nothing between them. She seemed to understand his situation better than he did. And if her boss had assigned her such a high-profile assignment, she had to be good at what she did.

If he thought of her as an assistant, not someone finding him dates, but someone arranging royal appearances of a sort, he would not merely get through this, the outings would do the job they were supposed to do. And his life could go back to normal.

He took a breath. "And what is my message?"

Pete turned to Rowan. "Rowan?"

Still holding his gaze, she said, "That you're a youthful king. Still strong. Still vital. Not merely able to lead but someone worthy of a position of prominence. Someone handsome, a good face of your country."

His heart fluttered a bit when she called him strong and vital and then handsome, but he ignored it.

"And how do you turn that into one-liners?"

"I don't. I write things like, 'Good morning, everyone, isn't it a beautiful day,' for you to say when you're walking to a limo with the woman I've chosen for you to take out. Then they'll subconsciously connect your sentiment about the day to your sentiment about your companion and they'll know you're fine."

It sounded so easy, like something that would weave into his life without much fanfare. It also sounded like a simple way to reassure his subjects without having to hold a press conference or issue a statement that *would* sound like he was making excuses.

It was the personification of actions speaking louder than words.

Pete said, "And that's it in a nutshell, Your Majesty. Now, if you'll excuse me, I have another meeting."

With that he left and Jozef was suddenly alone with Rowan. The silent room vibrated with possibilities, as they held each other's gaze. The attraction he didn't want to feel for her tightened his chest. But he was too old for her and she had a job to do. If she did it right, he could get out of this blip of trouble without making it into a big deal.

Rowan set her napkin beside her untouched plate of food and pushed back her chair. "I'm going to get started with some research. Do you want to meet this afternoon?"

Telling himself to just do it and get it over with, he said, "Yes. I'll see you this afternoon."

Then he watched her leave. Confusing emotions rattled through him. He couldn't believe he hadn't seen how his actions would worry his subjects, but he hadn't. He also couldn't believe he was attracted to a woman closer to his sons' ages than his own. But he was.

Luckily dignity and pride came to his rescue. He would humble himself to alleviate the fears of his subjects. And he would not make things worse by salivating over a woman who was too young for him. He wouldn't disrespect his position or his late wife that way.

Rowan drove back to work, forcing her mind to go over choices of eligible women who could be potential dates for a king. There was a glamorous American actress in her forties who—like Jozef—looked no older than thirty-five. Sterling, Grant, Paris also had a client who was a princess from a neighboring country. She'd gotten a bad deal when her husband was caught cheating and divorced her. The whole world would probably love to see her on a date with a handsome man, a king no less. That would put Princess Helaina's cheating spouse in his place. And if Rowan really wanted to get bold, she could set Jozef up with a billionaire tech genius, who sometimes used Sterling, Grant, Paris's services. That would be great for *Jozef's* image. He wouldn't merely be dating a pretty woman, he'd be dating someone who was smart and savvy enough to run one of the biggest companies in the world.

Taking the elevator to the third-floor temporary office suite Sterling, Grant, Paris had rented for this job, she decided the tech genius was definitely in the running, but she had to be the second or third date. Not first. The first date had to be casual, maybe a soccer game, with the American actress. She was beautiful, smart and fun, and they could look like two friends who had connected over a mutual love of soccer. The tech genius could be second. The Princess would be third. By then the public would be accustomed to seeing Jozef out on dates again, and they'd be hoping for him and the Princess to connect for real. Maybe date long-term—

Or even get married! What a royal treat that would be for all of Europe! She could see the press coverage now. It would be magnificent.

Pride rippled through her, but it was followed by the oddest jolt of regret. She was marrying off a man she found both interesting and tempting. A good-looking man who was intelligent and in control. A guy who would clearly be fascinating on a date and amazing after the date, when they'd go back to his place and—

She shook her head to stop the roll of her imagination. What the hell was she thinking? Dear Lord. This was a client! And she was a rising star on the verge of starting her own firm. Plus, one humiliating breakup was enough to keep her away from relationships forever.

Thinking of the betrayal—not just her fiancé but her best friend—soured her stomach. She'd believed the sun rose and set on Cash. She could picture their future children. They had a house together and a mortgage. All that spelled commitment to her. All that gave her reason to trust him. And he'd tossed her away, along with her ability to trust, because her best friend had seduced him?

What a load of rubbish. The fact that he hadn't been able to resist her was just another way of saying Rowan wasn't good enough.

Not able to stay in her small West Virginia town after her great humiliation, she'd moved to New York City, where she'd gotten a job as an assistant in a public relations firm. She'd climbed the ladder with relative ease because she was a natural at finding the right thing for a client to say or do to get out of a jam. Then she was lured to Europe to work for Sterling, Grant, Paris. Five years later, she was at the top of the heap and married to her job. No one would ever hurt her again. But she'd also use her life to make sure people who had been hurt could raise their heads with dignity and grace after their own great humiliations.

She was going to help King Jozef. The way he hadn't even noticed he was in trouble was proof that he needed her, and that always touched her heart.

Plus, her success was going to be public. Her name might not be on the lips of every average citizen, but people in PR circles would see this and understand she had "the goods." People who needed assistance clearing their names or getting back into the world again would also see her work, and her name would be the one they'd think of when they needed help.

Which was why the minute the job with Jozef was done, she had to leave Sterling, Grant, Paris and strike out on her own.

It would be her opportunity to shine, and, by God, she was taking it.

As she walked through her assistant's workspace into her office, Geoffrey scrambled from his seat, following her.

"So?"

She shrugged out of her jacket. "So what?"

"Oh, my God, you met a king! *The King.* Of an entire country. How did it go?"

"Yesterday, not so well. Much better this morning." She didn't tell him that she'd gazed into the King's dark eyes—beautiful eyes made sexy by the brooding secrets behind them. She didn't tell him that for a minute she thought she'd felt something pass between them. Not only was she the worst judge of character when it came to romance, but also the guy she'd shared the moment with was a king. She was as common as they came. The thought of them being together was… wrong.

She sat on the tall-back chair behind the unusually high stack of paper on her desk. "What is all this?"

"Phone messages and emails I printed out. Everybody in Convenience, West Virginia wants you to come home for your dad's surprise birthday party."

A shiver of revulsion rippled through her. She thought of the day her fiancé had arrived at her parents' house with her best friend and they'd told her they'd gotten married, thought of her wedding gown still hanging in the closet of her old bedroom, thought of how quiet Convenience, West Virginia had sounded that night, as if everyone was walking on tiptoe, embarrassed for her.

With humiliation riding her blood, she pretended indifference. "Seriously? Why do this many people care?"

"You know your mom wants *all* her kids home for the party."

And part of her wanted to go. Her parents had visited her in New York and even traveled to Europe for her birthday last year. She missed them.

The other part liked the woman she'd become outside of her small town. She didn't want to revert to the naive twenty-two-year-old who'd been so blinded by love she hadn't seen the signs that her fiancé was cheating.

That part won. "I'll be busy with the King."

"But the party's the end of next month. Eight weeks from now. I thought this was a six-week gig?"

"It might run a little longer." Forcing her mind off Convenience and onto the assignment, she tapped her fingers against her lips. "We have to get King Jozef somewhere significant every other week for a month. Then that opens the door for us to set him up with Princess Helaina."

Geoffrey gasped. "Princess Helaina?"

She grinned, though something inside her felt weird again at setting Jozef up to fall in love with another woman. "I know. We'll be killing two birds with one stone. Get him out in public and make it look like our poor embarrassed princess has moved on from her cheating husband. Then a nice six-week relationship for them proves they're both over their troubles, and they can break up like normal people and look like healthy individuals."

She frowned at the way her scenario now had them breaking up. Still, it worked.

"You're a genius."

"No. I'm really sort of wishful thinking here. It will take us the whole month to get the public accustomed to seeing Jozef again without making a big deal out of it. If that works, we'll call dating Helaina his Phase II."

Geoffrey shook his head. "I still think it's genius. I'll leave you alone to work your magic."

He walked away and she picked up the phone. She had to get an American actress to Prosperita without it looking staged.

CHAPTER THREE

AT THE END of the day, King Jozef strode down the marble corridor that led to his official office. Though he did most of his work in the private office in his suite, all meetings were handled here. He had about ten minutes until his sons were to arrive. Enough time to check his messages and figure out how he would tell his children to butt the hell out of his life.

He walked inside the workspace of his assistant, Nevel, who had apparently gone for the day, and plucked up the stack of yellow slips of paper, messages Nevel had taken that day.

Reading the messages, Jozef continued into the ornate office with velvet drapes, Oriental rugs and the massive mahogany desk of the original King of Prosperita that was over five hundred years old.

About to take his seat, he glanced up, and there, bolder than life, was Rowan Gray, sitting on the chair across from the big desk.

Her black suit was a bit rumpled, but her stunning green eyes were bright, shining.

Ignoring the jolt of attraction, he scowled. “Don’t you ever call ahead or make appointments? Or do you just barge in everywhere?”

“I work for you now. And I’m told my business with you is top priority.”

“Don’t you have another client you could be annoying?”

“You’re my main project, Your Majesty.”

The way she said *Your Majesty* made his nerve endings crackle. He cursed in his head and once again had to admit his sons might be right. For him to be so attracted to a stranger who was all wrong for him, it must be time for him to get out into the world again.

“I’ve arranged an outing for you.”

He closed his eyes and sighed. “Opera? Symphony? Grocery store opening?”

She laughed. “Nothing so trite.”

“You want me to be the grand marshal for a parade?”

“We discussed you going on *dates*, remember?”

Of course, he remembered. Having a stranger choose women to accompany him to events reminded him of his teen years, when Castle Admin would suggest possible young ladies for him to date. It had been both embarrassing and overwhelming. That was part of why he and Annalise had asked their parents to arrange their marriage. Having the press following his every move and a stranger find him dates brought back that horrible feeling.

He settled into the tall leather-backed chair behind his desk.

"I have you meeting Julianna Abrahams at a soccer game on Friday."

His head snapped up. When Rowan talked about finding dates for him, he always pictured dowagers in orthopedic shoes. Julianna Abrahams was every man's fantasy.

One of his eyebrows quirked. "Julianna Abrahams?"

"She's pretty and smart and very funny. She was a client of mine a few years back. She owed me a favor and agreed to fly here and be your date."

His happiness nosedived. "Exactly what every man wants. For a pretty girl to think he needs a PR firm to get him dates."

"She doesn't think that. I told her I thought being with you could boost both of your images. She saw the point."

He snorted. "You didn't make me look pathetic?"

"Oh, Your Majesty. You are far from pathetic.

You are extremely strong. It's simply time for us to remind everybody of that."

He felt the wave of attraction to her roll through him again and this time it was harder to ignore, but he managed.

"Plus, I'm trying to bolster your reputation, not make you look worse." She paused only a second before she added, "Julianna is great. And you like soccer."

"Football."

She winced. "Sorry. I know you guys call it football. But what we call your outing is beside the point. The point is she's perfect for you. Who knows? You might hit it off for real."

"And then you'd leave?" He'd said it sarcastically, but disappointment flooded him. How could that be when he had a date with America's Sweetheart? Just the thought of going out with Julianna Abrahams should dismiss his attraction to Rowan—

Shouldn't it?

Of course, it should!

So why hadn't it?

"I stay until your press is filled with pictures of you smiling at happy subjects."

He snorted in derision, but he looked at his watch and realized that any second his sons would be arriving for their meeting.

Needing to get rid of her, he rose from his

seat. "Okay. Great. Email the particulars for the date with Julianna to my assistant Nevel in the morning." He walked around the desk and motioned for her to rise.

She gave him a puzzled look but stood up and turned to the door just as his sons entered.

Everybody stopped dead in their tracks as Liam and Axel stared at Rowan, and Jozef felt like a trapped rat. Though he had no idea why. He had legitimate business with Rowan. And they couldn't read his mind and see he was attracted to her.

Blond-haired, blue-eyed Liam recovered first. Stepping forward he offered her his hand. "I'm Liam. I hope we didn't interrupt anything."

"Ms. Gray was just leaving."

Axel, who was the image of Jozef when he was younger with his dark hair and eyes, also offered his hand to Rowan. "I'm Axel."

Jozef almost groaned when he held Rowan's hand a tad too long. The little player was going to hit on her!

"Okay. That's enough." He guided Rowan away from his sons. "I'll be waiting for the particulars once you give them to Nevel."

She said, "Okay," and he closed the door on her before she could say anything else.

Liam said, "Who is she?"

Jozef strode to his desk. "Really, you don't

know the PR person I'm told you begged Castle Admin to hire?"

"I wouldn't say we begged," Axel said with a laugh, his straight shoulder-length black hair shifting as he moved.

Liam had the good graces to look sheepish. "We simply suggested that you needed to be seen in public more."

"And this is your business because..."

"Because you're not yourself. You've been giving all your events to either me or Liam," Axel said, sliding his hip onto the corner of his dad's desk. The casual way he behaved reminded Jozef of all the times he'd had the boys in his office when they were toddlers, then little boys, then teenagers. They'd thrown baseballs. Played tag. Played board games. He'd never wanted them to feel unwelcome in his office. More than that, though, he'd wanted Liam, heir to throne, to feel like this was where he belonged.

He suddenly missed those days, missed his sons as boys. He missed showing them the world with their mother. Then he missed their mother. Briefly, like a shadow crossing his soul, he felt the loss of the woman who'd helped him rule their country.

Jozef quietly said, "I'm training you to take my place."

Liam laughed. "Seriously? You think I need twenty years to learn to run a country?"

"You think you don't?"

Liam frowned. Axel relaxed negligently on the desk. As the non-heir, he didn't have a care in the world. But he liked supporting his brother. He enjoyed his royal duties. If he wasn't such a badass with women, he'd be the perfect child.

No. He wasn't a child anymore. Or even a teenager acting out because he missed his mother. He was a man. And maybe his sons were feeling as adrift as his subjects felt because their dad had all but become a hermit.

"Why don't we do something tonight?"

Axel glanced over at him. "Us? The three of us?"

Jozef nodded.

Axel said, "Like what?"

"Why don't we go to the media room and watch a game?"

Liam sniffed. "It's probably already started."

"Who cares? Let's just go. We'll call the kitchen and have them make junk food."

They headed for the door and Jozef's world didn't exactly right itself. He still felt the pang of emptiness that always rose when he thought of Annalise. But he had spent the past year in a sort of no-man's-land. His boys had grown up and he was feeling alone.

Watching a soccer game together might be just what they all needed.

On Friday, video conferencing with her staff in Paris about other clients took most of Rowan's day. She found herself racing to the castle less than a half hour before Josef would be leaving for the soccer game and his date with Julianna.

By the time she got through the security gate and pulled up to the huge gray stone castle, his limo was already by the door he would use to exit. Grabbing the polo shirt Pete had asked her to buy to assure Jozef looked comfortable and relaxed on his date, she scrambled to the limo, showed her credentials to the driver and slid into the back seat.

Josef came out of the door, and she groaned. Wearing jeans and a white shirt with the collar open, he at least had one part of the outfit right. But he looked so out of touch with reality that she groaned again.

He approached the limo, and the driver opened the door. Not noticing her, he slid inside. When he saw her sitting right beside him, he started. "What are you doing here?"

She ignored his question and clicked her tongue. "Really? Jeans and a white shirt for a sporting event?"

"You're in a suit!"

"I know but I'm working. I'm not going to a soccer game."

"*Football* game! It's *football* here. And you *are* on your way to the game. That's where the limo is taking us."

She retrieved the bag from beside the seat and pulled out the red and blue striped shirt. "Here."

He looked at it then looked at her. "What's this?"

"Your new, more comfortable, more relaxed shirt. My boss apparently saw pictures of you from a game a couple of years ago, and he didn't like what you were wearing."

He rolled his eyes. "Well, we certainly can't have that, can we?"

"Come on. This is my job and my boss's job. The shirt might seem like a small thing, but we want you to look young and approachable. Just one of the guys going to a soccer game with a pretty girl."

He said, "It's football," but he took the shirt.

The scowl on his face told her he wasn't happy. When he didn't make a move to change shirts, she said, "Go ahead. Put it on."

"Over my shirt?"

She laughed. He was deliberately being difficult, but she refused to take the bait. She'd handled worse clients. "Remove the shirt. And put on the casual, comfortable, shirt."

"In here? Right now?"

"Oh, come on. I'll bet you've changed in a limo before."

He frowned.

"Please?"

Something shifted in his eyes. He hesitated, looking at the shirt, then at her. With a disgruntled sigh, he dropped the striped shirt to the space between them on the limo seat, unbuttoned his white shirt and slipped it off, leaving him in his undershirt, which he yanked over his head.

Rowan plucked the polo from the seat and turned to hand it to him, but her gaze collided with his bare shoulders, chest and abdomen. Very flat abdomen. She successfully kept herself from reacting, but she couldn't deny she'd been checking him out and he'd probably seen.

As the garment went from her to him, their hands brushed and their eyes met. Electricity crackled between them. She wasn't just attracted to him. *He* was attracted to her.

Which was wrong.

For them both.

He was a client. Off-limits. And a *king*.

Plus, it was her job to get him out in public again on *dates* with other women. Following up on this thing between them would be self-sabotage.

She cleared her throat and turned away. "Hurry up! Get that shirt on. We'll be at the entry to your private tunnel to the stands in a few minutes."

He shrugged into the polo shirt, but he kept his gaze on her face as if confused. After a few seconds, he grinned like a Cheshire cat.

Damn it! She might have done her best to brush away her attraction, but he'd seen her reaction. He now knew she was attracted to him.

She could feel her face reddening and cursed herself. She wasn't a twelve-year-old girl. She shouldn't have stared when he took off his shirt. She couldn't even appear to be interested in him on any level but professional.

Hell, she wasn't *allowed* to be interested in him.

He. Was. A. Client.

CHAPTER FOUR

THE LIMO SLID through the gates leading to the private tunnel that would take Jozef to an elevator that would stop right beside the royal box. Neither he nor Rowan spoke as they rode to the second floor. When they reached the royal box, she set her fingers on the forearm of the security guard who had moved to open the door.

"One second."

Her focus back on the job where it belonged, she straightened Jozef's collar, then bunched the loose shirtsleeves to his elbows, making him look casual, relaxed. "Just be yourself."

"Sure," he said, but he grinned at her again.

Men. Even accidentally hint that you might be attracted to them, and they got all proud and goofy.

Yet another reason to keep everything professional with this guy.

"You might not believe this, Rowan. But I'm

actually friends with world leaders. I've met a movie star or two. You don't have to babysit me."

She shook her head, then caught the gaze of the security guard who opened the door. Her PR instinct shot to high alert when she saw Jozef's sons standing by the wet bar, with Julianna Abrahams, chatting her up.

Liam said, "Dad! Look who's here."

Okay. The first thing she had to do was get rid of his sons. She couldn't really think of a way to do that that wouldn't alert the press something was up in the royal box—

Of course, that might work in her favor. There *was* something happening in the royal box. King Jozef had a date. She wanted the press to see that.

Before she could say or do anything, Josef walked over to Julianna and offered his hand to shake hers. "Excuse my sons. They sometimes forget their manners. It's a pleasure to meet you."

Julianna shook his hand, her blue eyes gleaming. She tucked a strand of long yellow hair behind her ear. "The pleasure is mine. Your sons are charming."

"*I'm* charming," Axel clarified, then he pointed at Liam. "He's a stuffed shirt because he's next in line to head the family business."

Julianna laughed. "Family business?"

Fully living up to his reputation as royal player, Axel shrugged. "Running the country goes from one of us to the next, down the line of succession. So, yeah. Family business."

That was about as much as Rowan intended to let Axel steal the show. "Shoo. Take your security detail and go sit in the stands. You're making this look like a family picnic instead of a date. It needs to look like a date!"

Julianna laughed. "You should listen to her," she told Axel and Liam. "She made me appear to be a saint when my ex left me." She smiled at Rowan. "Kept me from having to pay millions to a guy who'd been nothing but a sponge."

The boys grumbled, but they left.

Jozef turned to Julianna. "Shall we sit?"

"Okay." She glanced around. "But I'm not sure how anybody's going to see we're together." She looked at Rowan. "Isn't that the point of this?"

"Yes, that is the point of this," Rowan said, but Jozef interrupted her.

"Don't worry. Photographers have long-range lenses."

Rowan took a few steps back. "Yes. They do. And we don't necessarily want them homing in on me." She inched back another few steps. "In fact, it's probably time for me to leave too. I'll go find your sons. Smooth things over. And make sure they don't say anything we don't want them to say. You two just enjoy the game."

She quickly exited and asked a security guard to help her find the two Princes. As it turned out, Castle Admin had two royal boxes, the second one obscure. In case the royals really did want privacy, they had it.

But before she stepped inside the room, she turned and faced the official royal box again. The picture of Jozef laughing with Julianna popped into her head and sent the strangest feeling cascading through her.

White-hot jealousy.

She grimaced. That was ridiculous. She found the guy attractive, sure. But probably half the people in the known universe did. The guy was hot. And that accent? Who wouldn't turn to mush hearing that? She was normal. There was nothing more to it than that.

Although it did suddenly hit her that Liam and Axel were closer to her age than their father, she didn't get those floaty, sometimes breathless feelings when they were around.

Which was another thing she refused to think about.

* * *

Jozef enjoyed his time with Julianna, who was bright and cheerful and accommodating. So unlike Rowan, who kept popping up out of nowhere, telling him what to do.

Seriously. He was a king. Her boss was smart enough to respect that. But Rowan? No. She just muscled her way into everything, insisting he do her bidding.

No one was supposed to tell him what to do. Advise? Sure. Tell him to take off his shirt and put on another, that was—

His breath stuttered.

"Are you okay?"

His gaze whipped to Julianna, who sat munching popcorn, enjoying the game.

"Yes. Sorry. Just thinking about things."

"Kingly duties?"

He was thinking about a woman he was attracted to and how she'd reacted when he took off his shirt. He was attracted to her and now he knew she was attracted to him. He'd seen that in her eyes when he'd removed his shirt.

"No. Not kingly duties. I can compartmentalize. And kingly duties are a lot like running a conglomerate. Though sometimes our parliament does get a bit pushy, I just think of them like the board of directors for a big company."

She smiled.

He waited to have a reaction to her. A twinkle of happiness. A shot of adrenaline. None came.

Disappointment fluttered up.

A week ago, none of this would have even registered in his mind. Now suddenly the whole country was worried about him, and he'd agreed with the PR firm Castle Admin had hired that letting them take the lead in getting him out socially was wise.

So here he was, on a date with Julianna Abrahams, when the woman he was attracted to was…

Off-limits. Wrong for him. Wrong for his image. Just plain wrong.

But she was also attracted to him.

The thought filled him with pleasure before it made him swallow hard.

His life would be a mess if he pursued her. Hell, she might not even want him pursuing her.

Otherwise, she would have flirted or something.

Wouldn't she?

Of course, she would have.

And that brought him back to Julianna Abrahams, sitting beside him in the royal box, watching a football game. He really was only forty-five. His wife was gone. It was time to get on with the rest of his life.

With Julianna engrossed in the game, he glanced around, wondering if this was what the next few years would be like as he either dated as a normal widower would or found a new wife—

No.

He couldn't even let his thoughts go that far. This was about dating like a normal widower.

If there was such a thing.

He pondered that for the rest of the game, then suddenly the final score was announced, and he'd missed it all.

The door opened and Rowan walked in. Her simple beige pantsuit made her look tall and slender. Her glorious red hair floated all around her. His gut clenched and his breath wanted to stutter.

He told his hormones to stop.

He had a country to think of. Not just himself. He might want to date like a normal widower, but he didn't think normal widowers dated hot thirty-year-olds.

That is…if she was even thirty years old.

He had no idea exactly how old she was. But were he to guess, it would be between twenty-eight and thirty.

Rowan said, "Axel and Liam are helping me get back to the castle, where I left my car. I'll see you tomorrow, Jozef."

The resignation that filled his brain as she walked away wasn't comforting. He had no intention of pursuing her. She'd let her attraction to him slip out that night, but she'd also immediately pulled back. Meaning, they were on the same page. They were two adults who appreciated each other, but nothing would come of it.

Saturday morning, the tabloids awaited him at the breakfast table. Two photographers had managed to get a shot of him kissing Julianna good-night—something he'd believed a necessity when they'd parted company to go to their respective limos.

Two got pictures of her racing to her car, as if trying to avoid paparazzi. Her not wanting people to see she'd had a date with a king only made it seem more real, not planned at all.

He chuckled. Julianna was better at this than she let on. And though he was loath to admit it, Rowan had been correct. Their date the night before had been good for them both.

His sons came to breakfast to talk about meeting Julianna but it seemed like every other sentence contained a reference to Rowan.

"I think we should keep her on speed dial," Liam suggested, "for when Axel does the monumental screwup we all know he's going to do eventually."

Axel snorted. Jozef shook his head, not even dignifying that with a comment. Particularly since his sons' need for him to get out in public had started all this.

He was considering dating again.

For real.

That was, after he had three dates with women Rowan chose for him.

It would have made him a bit queasy, except he'd taken a second marriage off the table. He wasn't there yet. Dating now would be for fun.

He really hadn't had any fun in his life in a long time.

Lost in thought, he strode into his office with purposeful steps only to stop dead in his tracks.

"What are you doing here?"

Seated in the chair behind his desk, Rowan turned to face him. "We'll be debriefing the morning after every date."

"Fabulous." She looked pretty and perky and this morning her full lips looked incredibly kissable. "But that doesn't explain what you're doing in my chair."

She winced. "I thought your breakfast with your sons would last longer." She winced again. "And I wanted to see if sitting in the chair of a king would make me feel any different."

Telling his wayward thoughts to take a hike, he crossed his arms on his chest. "Did it?"

She glanced around as if confused. "Actually no."

"Do I have to count to ten to get you out or should I call security?"

She bounced out of the chair. "Sorry."

He waited until she rounded the desk, then he walked behind it and took his seat. "Second order of business, there is nothing to debrief about. The *date* was nice. Made me realize just how much I had been keeping myself at home and decide I really do want to get out more. And now I am fine. I can finish this on my own."

She chuckled and sat on the chair in front of his desk. "Funny stuff, Your Majesty. Especially since you know we're only in phase one. Your next date is with Paula Mason."

He thought for a second. "The tech genius?"

She smiled. "Yep."

His brain should have produced a picture of a blonde beauty with a brain as fast and accurate as the software she created, but it suddenly homed in on the fact that Rowan wasn't in a pantsuit. She wore a tight skirt and a floaty blouse that set off the color of her hair but was also extremely feminine.

"Speechless, right?"

He sort of was. Not because of Paula, but because he was not the kind of guy who noticed women's clothing. Sure. If someone had on a miniskirt or a bikini, he saw. He wasn't an idiot. But who the hell cared if someone's blouse complemented their hair? Well, apparently, he did, since he'd noticed.

"This date's going to go like this. Not this Friday, but next Friday afternoon, she'll come to the castle to meet with you and some of the members of your advisory council to talk business."

Confused, he frowned. "Business?"

"The future of...you know, computers and the internet and your country's place in that world, or maybe what you need for infrastructure to meet demand. Then you'll both come out of the castle dressed for an evening out. There's a gallery opening. Castle Admin arranged for you to go in an hour before the normal crowd is permitted to enter. I want the press to see her getting out of your limo in something glamorous..." She peered up at him. "You'll be in a tux. You'll spend an hour or so in the gallery, then it's back in the limo and to a restaurant for dinner."

That did not sound like fun. It sounded scripted and overscheduled...

Still, this wasn't the rest of his life. All Rowan

got was three dates to show his subjects he was fine, and he should look at those dates as practice for when he started getting himself out into the world again. Better to mess up with women he wasn't really interested in than the ones he'd choose for himself.

"Okay. Fine."

"I'll be checking on your wardrobe."

He sighed. "I wear a suit for meetings, and you already said I'd be wearing a tux for the gallery opening."

"Sounds good." She snapped her leather notebook closed and rose. "We'll talk next Thursday."

He also rose. "The day before the date?"

"Yep. We can go over anything you want. Then we'll debrief Saturday morning."

And he wouldn't see her until then? No more having her pop up in his office or spin around in his office chair?

That was for the best. Actually, it was smart.

With that, she turned to go and Jozef watched her leave, surprised at the disappointment that consumed him. He sat down, prepared to work, but he couldn't. Everything felt off. Wrong somehow.

A week ago, he was a man who enjoyed his privacy. Then a gorgeous public relations woman came into his life, and he realized his subjects were worried about him. Wanting to alleviate their fears, he agreed to go out with a movie star. On that date, he realized she wasn't his cup of tea, but he was ready to get out into the world again.

To date.

He'd been content to be a solitary widower. Now suddenly, he was thinking about dating—

Attracted to Rowan—

Feeling alone in his castle quarters—

How the hell had this happened?

He threw his pen down on his desk and strode out of his stuffy, stifling office and into his assistant's workspace.

"Tell Castle Admin I'll be at the stables. I've decided to take the day to do some riding."

Nevel stood up nervously. "But you have two meetings—"

"Cancel them."

Rowan left his office completely flummoxed. The meeting had gone well, but there was something about Jozef that struck her as funny. She got the weird sensation of spiders crawling down her spine, the way she always did when a client was about to do something stupid—

But that was crazy talk. Jozef was as controlled as a guy could get. He wasn't about to do a striptease on the bar of a tavern the way one of her rock star clients had or race his motorcycle down Ventura Boulevard, taking cops on a four-mile, high-speed chase. He understood that he had to keep his reputation solid.

Still, sometimes when a PR firm came in and began planning a person's life, they could feel too controlled and rebel. As much as logic would tell the client that the PR plan was correct, they'd feel stifled…and do something stupid to wrestle back control.

And this guy was a king. The definition of *stupid* expanded exponentially for him. Rock stars and movie stars were given tons of leeway before anybody marked their actions as foolish. Josef had simply withdrawn and his subjects got nervous. God only knew what would happen if he did something that really was wrong.

The feeling of spiders using her spine as a superhighway intensified. She had to do something.

She tried calling him that afternoon, but he didn't answer his phone.

His assistant refused to give her any information about his whereabouts.

Castle Admin informed her he'd simply taken an afternoon off and there was nothing to worry about.

But years of experience with clients told her she was right. Something was up with Jozef.

She tried to picture him riding a motorcycle like a rocket down the streets of Prosperita's capital city and ended up with hives.

The more she thought about their ten minutes together that morning, the more she realized he'd definitely had the look of a guy who was going to burst, and technically this was her job: see the signs of a meltdown and prevent it.

She left her office, hopped into her SUV and raced to the castle. She got past security and two butlers but was told Jozef wasn't there.

"I'll wait," she said, nosing around the wide hallway outside his private quarters, as the butler blocked the door.

"This is highly irregular."

"You do know I'm his PR person, right? I'm supposed to look at his life, figure things out and change whatever is wrong. I can't do that if I'm on the outside looking in, can I?"

The weathered butler sighed. "No, ma'am, I suppose you can't."

"Call Castle Admin— No wait. I'll do it." She picked up her phone and hit the speed dial number for Art Andino. When he answered, she put the call on speaker. "Art, this is Rowan. I need to speak with Jozef and he's not in his quarters. I needed to talk to him ASAP. Like the second he gets home. I could wait in the sitting room for his residence, but his butler wants me to leave and come back later. And that means, I won't get to talk to him the second he gets home."

"Let her in the sitting room, Raphael," Art replied, obviously recognizing the call was on speaker.

The butler said, "Yes, sir."

He motioned for her to enter, then disappeared.

She closed the door behind her. "Thanks, Art."

Art sighed. "Just don't go beyond the sitting room… And don't touch anything."

Five minutes later, the butler was back asking if she wanted tea while she waited.

Having skipped lunch, she said, "Tea would be nice."

Then she glanced around the residence of her client and itched to get beyond the front room. She really should look for clues about what was going on with this guy.

Of all of her clients, *he* was the one who really could not afford to make a mistake.

Peering at the antiques and big portraits of former kings, all of whom looked as controlled as Jozef, she realized she could be overreacting. Jozef was accustomed to being in the public eye. He was also mature, intelligent and majestic—

Oh, boy. If she'd gotten this wrong, if he wasn't about to melt down, he would be furious with her when he came back and found her in his sitting room.

CHAPTER FIVE

WHEN THE OBJECT of her fears finally walked into his residence, he wore a T-shirt and jeans and boots that looked like hiking boots. Tall and lean, just muscled enough to be sexy, with his dark hair disheveled, he gave new meaning to the word *masculinity.*

She struggled with a moment of pure lust, but quickly regained control. "Where have you been?"

She asked pleasantly because she didn't want to offend him, make him feel cornered or get fired.

"I wanted a break. And I took one. I think the bigger question is why are you in my private quarters?"

"Castle Admin authorized it. I went looking for you and when I couldn't find you, they allowed me to wait for you here." She paused for a second, then added, "But they didn't tell me where you were."

He snorted. "I was on a horse. Riding. Just taking a normal break."

Oh, that accent.

Seeing him at his most masculine and hearing that voice made her want to curl up beside him on a big bed with satin sheets.

But she knew better. Especially given that he was her *client*.

"And you felt you needed a little horse therapy because..."

He sucked in a long breath. "Because of something that's none of your business."

"Everything about you for the next six weeks is my business. It's why Castle Admin hired me and why they let me see you anytime I want. For the next six weeks, *you* are my job. Why did you feel you needed a break?"

Clearly frustrated, he stared at the ceiling, his hands planted on slim hips that looked so damned fine in blue jeans.

Finally, he glared at her. "I should kick you out, but I know you'd only be in my office tomorrow morning asking the same questions. So let me save us both some trouble. All this attention on my private life has me feeling things that I needed to deal with."

Alleluia! Now they were getting somewhere.

"That's perfectly normal! When someone has to call in a public relations firm, it's usually because there's an issue in their life that caused them to feel they needed help with their image. In your case, you withdrew." She smiled again. "So, what kind of things were you feeling today?"

He gaped at her. He'd spent hours riding, grooming his stallion and thinking, as he mucked the stall to continue doing physical things in the hope his antsy feeling would go away. Ultimately, he'd realized dating didn't bother him as much as the up-and-down feelings he'd been having around Rowan.

She was brash, bold and running his life, yet he wanted to kiss her. And that was the real conundrum. She didn't see that *she* was the problem. And he wasn't about to tell her.

"Are you seriously asking me to tell you my feelings? Like you're a therapist? Good God, woman! Will you leave me with at least some semblance of dignity!"

"I'm not asking to be nosy. I'm asking because I can probably help. Odd feelings are normal when another person starts interfering in your life. No matter that I'm here to help and the things we'll do over the next few weeks will settle a few of your problems. It's still an intrusion. I've dealt with this before."

He sighed. He knew she was talking about

typical frustration a person would have when a PR person started changing things, but he envisioned every one of her clients being attracted to her.

Unfortunately, that only made him feel more common, less kingly. So far out of his comfort zone, it frustrated him to hell and back. "Great."

"It *is* great because I have seen this hundreds of times and handled it a bunch of different ways. I can probably tell you how to fix it." She smiled briefly, clearly trying to reassure him. "What are you feeling?"

He shook his head. He knew she wouldn't let this go unless or until he threw her something. Plus, if he couched his issue in generic terms, maybe they could figure out a way to dismiss it.

"All right. You asked for it. On the off chance you really can help… I'm feeling an odd surge of frustration that borders on anger."

"That's good! See? Getting it out in the open like that means we can deal with it."

"Or it means you can put it in a sappy press release that garners sympathy but makes me look like a fool."

She gasped. "I wouldn't do that."

"Right." He shook his head. "You'll do what you need to do."

"I *need* for you to continue looking healthy and strong not sappy. I won't be doing anything that makes you look sappy."

"Don't placate me. No matter how much you try to pretend to be my buddy, this job is just a job to you. You'll do whatever you deem appropriate in the moment."

She stayed silent awhile, then eventually said, "Is that what this is? You don't trust me?"

"Why should I?"

"Because my reputation is on the line here every bit as much as yours is. Don't tell anyone, but I'm this close to leaving Sterling, Grant, Paris to start my own firm. If the whole world sees I made you look wimpy, I might as well go back to West Virginia and crochet scarfs and mittens for a living. It's a black mark on my résumé if your subjects stop worrying about you because I made them feel sorry for you."

A weird sense of balance settled over him. It shocked him that she'd confided one of her secrets. But in the most unexpected way it had shifted his feelings about dealing with her. Her reputation would suffer if she botched this.

Suddenly the whole deal didn't feel so one-sided.

Unfortunately, knowing that did absolutely nothing to alleviate his attraction to her. It might have even made his desire to kiss her stronger.

"You know what you need to do?"

He peered over at her in her pretty skirt and floaty blouse. "What?"

"You need to do something just for yourself."

"I did. I went horseback riding."

She shook her head and walked over to him. "No. You need to get crazy. Do something that's out of the ordinary, maybe even against the rules."

"Horseback riding wasn't on my schedule. Nevel had to cancel two meetings."

She shook her head. "Wow. If you consider that crazy, your life really is dull."

The statement went through him like a shock wave of realization. His life *was* dull. Predictable. And maybe that was at the bottom of all this confusion? He worked so hard to conform, to do everything right, that now that he'd hit a level of perfection—good kids, strong country, solid economy, not a skeleton in his closet—he'd stopped living, as a way to protect it all.

The surprise of seeing that was so strong, he almost had to sit. No wonder his subconscious was revolting. No wonder her suggestion to do something crazy unexpectedly sounded right.

He was tired of his life being dull.

"Plus, horseback riding is still kingly. You need to do something un-kingly. Something no one expects. But do it in private..."

His brow furrowed. "Somewhere no one sees?"

"Yes. Exactly. Somewhere no one can see. So no one knows. No ramifications. It's your little secret."

His gaze dropped to her lush mouth. "My secret?"

"No one has to know."

He stepped away from her, calling himself insane for the temptation flitting through his brain.

She laughed. "Come on! I know there's something in there." She tapped his temple. "There's something you want to do." Her eyes brightened. "Do it."

Oh, hell. She could not know she was persuading him to kiss her...

Could she?

Maybe she did? He'd seen she was attracted to him. And it was just a kiss.

Plus, now that his confusion had broken and he realized he'd boxed himself into the most boring life possible, he was ready to be normal again.

To do what he wanted.

To be himself.

He caught her by the shoulders and simultaneously stepped closer as he pulled her to him. His mouth met hers quickly, not giving her a chance to protest, and a bolt of electricity matched the roar of thunder that sizzled through him.

She'd been correct.

This was exactly what he needed.

He could have stopped the kiss after a few seconds, but when her surprise wore off, she relaxed against him, and her hands slid to his shoulders.

His hands slid down her slim back and leisurely rose to her shoulders again.

Their mouths opened.

The kiss deepened.

For the next thirty seconds, pure bliss billowed through him. Then arousal rolled in. He wanted to take the kiss to the next level. He wanted it so much he almost couldn't believe the thoughts bouncing around like popcorn in his brain.

He struggled to remind himself that this was just supposed to be a kiss. A fun, quasi-rebellious thing to make him feel like himself again, but this was as far from his real self as he'd ever been, as wants and needs collided and took over.

He wrestled control back again and stepped back. With his hands still on her shoulders, he watched her pretty green eyes open and blink once.

"Was that risky enough for you?"

He made the joke only because he wasn't ready to face the things rumbling through him. His marriage to Annalise had been arranged by his parents, and though they'd had a fabulous sex life and a wonderful marriage, he'd never felt this kind of roaring, growling, hunger.

It had to be wrong.

She cleared her throat and stepped back too. "Well. Okay. I mean… I didn't expect that your risqué thing would be with me. But… Well, wow."

Desire blasted through him. It was thrilling to know she'd liked the kiss as much as he had. But in the next breath he faced a million commonsense reasons why what he'd just done was wrong.

Wrong.

It might have been right because it jarred him out of his apathy. But it was wrong on all other levels possible.

"I'm sorry."

She held up a hand. "Oh. No. No. Don't be

sorry. I wasn't offended. I'm not exactly sure what's happening here but we can sort it out."

"I've wanted to kiss you since I met you."

Relief fluttered through her. That hadn't been a default kiss. He hadn't kissed her because she'd pushed him to do something risky and she was the only risky thing available. But that opened another door. Their mutual attraction had resulted in one hell of a kiss. For every bit as much as that filled her with bubbly joy, it was totally inappropriate.

"Okay. This is on me. I told you to do something slightly on the rebellious side and that kiss was it." Just saying that out loud stole her breath. She took a second to pull herself together. Then she realized he was perfectly calm. Talking like a sane person. He'd all but melted her bones and he barely seemed affected.

That realization worked to bring her down to earth until she remembered that for at least a couple of days, she'd been his fantasy kiss. She'd been the fantasy kiss of a *king*. A gorgeous, smart, sexy king.

Stop that! You have a job to do. One blistering kiss isn't going to ruin it.

Sensible King Jozef broke the silence. "But we can't do it again."

"Oh…no." She held up her hand as she singsonged. "We absolutely can't."

"Still, it was pretty good."

"Yup." *Maybe too good.*

He laughed. "You were right. That did make me feel better."

She took a few steps backward, inching toward the door, wanting to put some distance between them. The conflicting feelings of happiness that she had been his fantasy kiss, and disappointment that he didn't want anything to do with her kept bumping into each other, creating a weird dichotomy. She should be glad he didn't want anything to do with her—

But that was some kiss.

Shoving her internal battle aside, she forced herself to do her job. "Let's look at it this way. You were struggling with the sense of being confined or hemmed in and you're not feeling that anymore."

She plucked her coat from the back of one of the chairs in his sitting room. It was one thing to properly identify what had happened. Quite another to hang out in a room with a guy who'd kissed her like Prince Charming, returned her glass slipper, then told her he didn't want her.

"I'll see you in the morning."

Still unaffected, he nodded.

She opened the door and ran into the hallway to race down the grand stairway, the drama of it keeping her Cinderella feelings alive. Her heart pounded and her knees were weak, but she pushed through the foyer and out the door. When she got into her rented SUV, she laid her head on the steering wheel.

The man could kiss.

But he didn't want to kiss her again and, technically, she was not allowed to kiss clients.

She comforted herself with the knowledge that it would never happen again and most likely they'd never talk about it. Still, thoughts of the kiss bubbled up the whole time she drove home, as she ordered takeout for her dinner and tried to watch TV.

She squeezed her eyes shut, telling herself she was crazy. She wasn't a hermit. She dated, and she always liked the people she went out with. Kissing them had been great too. But there was something different in Jozef's kiss. And in the silence of her rented apartment, she let herself admit that what she'd felt was that spark people talked about. The spark that said there was something here. A bigger, better attraction. An attraction that meant something—

The same spark she hadn't felt since cheating Cash.

That tossed a barrel of water on the fantasy that wanted to blossom in her brain. Cheating Cash from Convenience, West Virginia. *Convenience, West Virginia.* Because that's where she was from. She was a small-town girl. Sure, she fit into the rarified world in which she worked because she was a really good schmoozer, but she was still an employee. Not one of the bigwigs.

She tried to picture herself as a queen and couldn't. Tried to picture Jozef in Convenience, West Virginia meeting her parents and couldn't.

But she could picture another broken heart. The absolutely horrible humiliation of having a king publicly dump her.

That would be the real end to anything that might happen between them. They wouldn't get married. She didn't have to worry about being a queen. They'd never mesh. Their lives would never entwine.

They would part.

Maybe that's what he meant when he said they couldn't kiss again.

Maybe that's what her brain had been trying to tell her when it continually reminded her he was a client.

They were not right for each other.

* * *

Monday morning, from her temporary office nowhere near the castle, she solidified the arrangements for Jozef's date with Paula Mason. She'd already told Jozef that they wouldn't have a strategy meeting until the day before the date, so there was no reason for her to go to his office, or even call him.

They would have over a week to forget their kiss. To let it fade into stardust and be blown away on an island breeze.

Which was exactly what needed to happen.

Hours later, she was ready to leave for the day when her cell phone rang with an unfamiliar number.

With a sigh, and a prayer it wasn't Jozef, she answered it.

CHAPTER SIX

JOZEF GATHERED THE hard copy of a trade agreement Liam had negotiated and headed out of his office. Everything inside him burst with pride. Liam might have hated that his father had begun to train him so he could someday fill the King's shoes, but training was a good thing.

Evidenced by the excellent agreement Liam had negotiated. His son was taking to the position of leader like a fish to water. And he was about to surprise him not just with a personal visit to his office, but also an abundance of praise.

He took the back corridor that led to the offices of both of his sons. But as he passed Axel's work area, Rowan stepped out, Axel right behind her, his hand on the small of her back.

Surprise hit him like a punch in the gut. All his muscles froze.

"Hey, Dad! Rowan's just agreed to help with the fall fundraiser."

"Oh." He let his gaze meander to her. Her face registered the same kind of shock that was rolling around in his belly. Excitement at seeing her mixed with trepidation. He didn't think she'd told his son that he'd kissed her. But he had kissed her and she had kissed him back.

The memory bloomed, bringing with it the flood of longing he'd been fighting for the past thirty-six hours. It didn't seem right that he should want her so badly when anything between them was totally inappropriate.

"Pete and I decided to look at it as an extension of the services we're rendering for you."

Not knowing what else to say, he mumbled, "That sounds fine."

He should have gone. Liam's office was only twenty or thirty feet away. He should have said, *If you'll excuse me, I'm on my way to see Liam*. But he couldn't seem to move. She'd raced out after he'd kissed her. But not before relieving him of any responsibility for it. Like a good PR person, she'd taken the blame, told him their blistering kiss was nothing but his need to get rid of some of his tension and clearly let him know she hadn't been affected.

Of course, he'd tried to salvage his pride by pretending the kiss had been nothing but logical. He couldn't grouse that she'd looked at it logically too.

Like the good employee she was.

The silence stretched out and just when he might have gotten his feet to move, he noticed that her long hair tumbled over a simple T-shirt, drawing his gaze to blue jeans and boots. He swallowed. She hadn't even worn blue jeans to their soccer game. What was she doing in jeans at a meeting—

With his son?

"We don't have clients come to the temporary office we set up, so lots of times we dress down," she explained, obviously having followed his line of vision.

Her gaze lifted to his.

His bones felt like they melted.

"So I'll see you next Thursday for the meeting before your date with Paula Mason."

Axel whistled. "Paula Mason! Dad! You are so lucky."

He didn't feel lucky. Instead, a little bit of his anger from the Saturday returned. He'd never disputed his responsibilities as King. He'd never been rebellious like Axel. He was more like Liam. In fact, he and Annalise had concocted the scheme to marry each other at only eighteen because finding a love match would have been a disaster with the press watching. After they'd married, they'd fallen in love.

And that, they'd decided, was the way things should be. As friends, they'd already known they were good for each other. Marrying, having love arise out of their friendship, worked better than the passion and uncertainty of romantic love.

Technically, he did not know this woman he was so damned attracted to. If they pursued what they felt, it would be clumsy.

Sexual.

Messy, because he'd never really understand what they were doing.

The thought of it was unexpectedly titillating, so he took a step away from her. Kings could not operate on whims and wishes. "I'm on my way to see Liam. Have a good evening, Rowan. Axel, maybe you and I should watch the game again tonight."

In the meeting with Rowan the day before his date with Paula Mason, Jozef was confident and commanding. Her normal procedure should be to explain the outing to him and ask if he had questions. That morning, he told her how things would go, then dismissed her in such a way she couldn't think of a reason to argue or stay. She returned to her office, finished her day and went home with takeout.

Though she was nervous about the date the next day, she forced her mind off Jozef and to her own future. With this assignment about half-done, it was time to consider the steps she'd be taking to start her own firm. She'd have to talk things over with Pete, of course, to get his blessing and hope he threw some overflow work her way until she had her own clientele.

But she also had some PR work to do for her new company. She'd have to create a campaign that announced that she was going out on her own. Especially in Manhattan. She'd chosen to go back to the States to make it easier for Sterling, Grant, Paris to recommend her to non-European clients.

And to get away from Jozef. The man had begun invading her dreams. She'd fallen asleep on the sofa the night after running into him outside Axel's office and dreamed of the episode just as it had happened, except everything suddenly morphed. Axel evaporated and the King didn't stutter or seem shellshocked. He'd taken her into his arms and kissed her—

She'd bounced up on the sofa, breathless and angry with herself, reminding herself they did not belong together.

Recalling the dream, she realized that was what his stiff and formal attitude that afternoon had been about. He might be attracted to her, but he wisely ignored those feelings. Cast them aside. Behaved like an adult.

She might be vacillating, but he wasn't.

The following afternoon she arrived at the castle to find all his cabinet members were already there. Slipping into the front foyer where Jozef stood congregating with twenty other men and women, she noticed he was the strong, self-assured ruler he had been at their meeting. Knowing he was fine, she worked to stay out of the way and simply let him be a strong, impressive king.

In fact, she was glad he was commanding and confident. Helping him come back into the world reflected well on her. He was becoming one of her success stories. He might have initially argued with her. He most certainly hadn't liked having her tell him what to do. But he hadn't had a big meltdown the way some of her clients did. He'd had a teeny tiny one that resulted in him kissing her.

Now he was ready to let go of whatever had been bothering him enough that he'd isolated and be the King he was.

She had done her job.

She should be proud.

She *was* proud.

But there was this niggling something in the back of her head that tried to ease out every once in a while, but it couldn't.

She'd think her hesitation or concern had something to do with Jozef, but he was great. Stronger than ever.

What the hell was it?

Finally, Paula's big, black limo pulled up in front of the castle, and she was escorted into the foyer. Wearing a slim blue pantsuit on her tall frame, she stepped forward, extending her hand to Jozef. Like Julianna Abrahams, she was blonde, but her hair was cut at the chin in a chic bob. Her mouth had lifted into a wide smile. Her blue eyes sparkled.

"It's a pleasure to meet you, Your Majesty."

Rowan's lips twisted as she tried to figure out why she always fixed him up with beautiful blue-eyed blondes. It was like she was saying she wasn't good enough. No redheads for the King. No women with lush figures.

No. That wasn't it. She'd chosen his dates with personality and impact in mind. Julianna Abrahams and Paula Mason were his level of stature.

Looks had nothing to do with it.

Satisfied with her explanation, she discreetly walked beside the assembled crowd of cabinet members and assorted executives of Paula's huge technology empire, as they made their way to a conference room.

It was like watching history in the making. His job was so serious, and he did it so well—

That was it! That was the weird thing tickling her brain.

His world was huge and filled with significance and consequence. That was true of all her clients in one way or another, but where movie stars and even corporate geniuses would fade into obscurity, historians would one day write about Jozef. Things he did, decisions he made, could someday change the fate of the world.

It was no wonder Castle Admin hired someone to make sure he stayed steady in the eyes of his subjects. He was important beyond the shores of his island. He was a world leader.

They reached the door to the huge conference room. Rowan would not be allowed to go beyond that point, but that was fine. She had other work to do.

Still, she couldn't stop watching him—

Jozef casually turned and caught her gaze.

She could have thought he was thanking her for doing a good job setting everything up with Paula. But the connection felt different. Personal.

Almost as if he'd wanted her to see *this* was his real world. Not the private times they'd had together when she'd bossed him and even sort of sassed him.

But the weight of who he was.

Was it a warning? Or an explanation.

The door closed behind him.

She stared at the polished wood. Memories of Convenience, West Virginia juxtaposed the scene of him with world leaders and the CEO of one of the biggest companies on earth.

She suddenly realized he was telling her that who he was made him different. Special. But also, he was a man who carried so much responsibility that he'd never be just a guy.

He was a king.

She was so common that she bought her undies at a big box store.

He'd wanted to kiss her because he found her attractive. But while she could dream about him, spin fantasies, there was no room in his life for something that would get him lambasted in the press—or, worse, in the eyes of the presidents, prime ministers and other royalty who were his peers.

Though the meeting with Paula Mason and her staff had been arranged as a way to get him seen out in public with her, Jozef made good use of the time. He picked her brilliant brain about her research and development and asked for advice on what his country needed to do to keep up with the times.

She was not shy about giving her opinion. A person did not get to her level of prominence by holding back. He not only respected that he used it to his advantage.

The trip to the gallery ended up being enjoyable and dinner was lighthearted and fun as she told him about growing up in upstate New York. Far away from where Rowan had been raised, but similar in terms of mountains and forests and small-town life.

Walking to his residence, he yanked off his tie and rolled his eyes. He knew his curiosity about the lifestyles in the different geographic regions of the United States was fueled by his forbidden curiosity about Rowan. But he had all that under control now.

Hadn't he been solid and all business in their meeting the day before his date? Of course he had been. Because he'd gone back to who he was: a leader. Not merely in charge of his own country but one of the rulers who would shape the world.

The next morning, he entered his office, expecting Nevel to tell him that Rowan was on her way over, or that she'd scheduled an appointment with him, but Nevel was nowhere around.

Then he remembered it was Saturday. Of course, Nevel wasn't around. Unless specifically asked to work, as he had been the week before, he took Saturdays and Sundays off.

He strode into his office. Nevel might not be working but Rowan surely would be. She said they would debrief after every date. And he'd had a date the day before. She wouldn't miss a chance to dig for every nitpicky detail.

Seconds later, she appeared at his door, takeout cup of coffee in hand.

He rose with a smile. "You don't have to bring your own coffee. I can have coffee here in under ten minutes."

She laughed. "I know. But I got up late, raced to dress and needed the caffeine boost as I was driving."

The normalcy of it made him laugh. Plus, she looked soft and happy in her jeans and boots, topped off by one of her fancy, floaty blouses.

He motioned to her chair. "Have a seat." Then a thought struck him. "Have you had breakfast?"

"No. I don't eat breakfast."

"Breakfast is the most important meal of the day!"

She shook her head as she approached the chair in front of his desk. "Not for me. Once I eat a carb, I want carbs for the rest of the day. I eat nothing but protein and fat until three or so. It's a tricky balance I have to maintain to keep my weight from climbing."

Again, the normalcy of the conversation, the simplicity of it, filled him with something he couldn't define or describe. He'd say it relaxed him, but it was more than that—

His chest tightened. *He was happy to see her.* No. He was happy to be alone with her. So happy, he almost felt giddy.

He drew a quiet breath, resurrecting the kingly demeanor he'd used the day before. "I'm sure you're here to get the details of my outing with Paula Mason."

She nodded, then took a sip of coffee.

"Everything was great. Paula's fabulous."

Their gazes met as her eyes filled with something that could have been disappointment. "You like her?"

He said, "Absolutely," but what he felt for Paula was so far removed from what he felt for Rowan it seemed wrong to let Rowan live with a deliberately misleading impression. He sighed. "I like her as a business associate. The woman's a genius. We had great conversations."

"Oh."

Her relief birthed corresponding relief in him. He recognized the road they were going down and stopped it before it really started. "And thanks to you, Prosperita now has a very strong ally. Someone who is willing to help us update technologically and maybe even put a satellite office here so we can keep more of our educated citizens on the island instead of having them move to Europe for work."

Pride filled her bright green eyes as her lips lifted into a smile. "That's great."

"It really is." Her surprise at his compliment reminded him that he'd barely let her know he'd appreciated everything she'd done for him. If he examined the slippery slope on which he'd been sliding before her firm stepped in, he realized he would have been a hermit in another few months.

She might not change the world the way Paula would, but in her own area of expertise, Rowan was as smart as Paula. Wearing jeans and a feminine shirt, with her hair in a bun, she also looked older than his sons. Actually, she looked like the hard worker he knew she was.

"I know I haven't been the best client, but you did a good job."

Her smile grew. "Thank you."

Wonderful warmth percolated through him.

But he caught it before it spilled over into the feelings he wasn't allowed to have.

"So that's it. Paula and I had a good time, made some deals, enjoyed each other's company."

"Okay. That one's in the books." She glanced down at her hands, then caught his gaze again. "One more date and you're free."

Her statement hung in the air. They both knew that after that date, he wouldn't see her again. In his entire life, he'd never felt what he did around her. And in a few weeks, it would be gone.

Not just her, but the chance.

Not to sleep with her. Not even to investigate the attraction. But to really be himself. To say what he wanted, knowing he wouldn't be judged. To laugh unrestrictedly. To give voice to the thoughts he sometimes had but didn't speak.

All because there was a spark of something between them. Something romantic and sexual. Something he'd always believed he didn't want suddenly tempted him.

He struggled for a witty comeback, but nothing came.

She sucked in a breath. "Actually, now that we're coming to the end of this, there are some things I have to tell you too."

The softness of her voice spoke of intimacy, trust. They'd scuffled and bantered, but they'd confided things. Been real with each other. He suddenly wondered if it hadn't been meeting her, rather than going on two random dates, that had forced him out of his doldrums.

"Watching you enter that conference room yesterday, I had a few 'aha' moments myself." She took another quick breath. "For one, I've treated you a little shabbily for someone who's a king."

He chuckled. "Really? You think so? I just thought all PR people were pushy and disrespectful. That that's how you got your work done."

She snorted. "That's basically true. Though not everybody has to get the cooperation of a king."

"Just the people looking to break out of the pack and start their own firm?"

She met his gaze. "We do have to prove ourselves."

He laughed again. He couldn't remember laughing this genuinely, this honestly, this comfortably in forever.

"Yesterday, I saw just how important you are."

Pride filled him, but it was replaced by a quick realization. He didn't have as much fun being important, as he did being himself. The truth of it froze him in place.

"I get it now. I looked at portraits along the walls of the main corridor, the people who ruled before you, and I realized this country has survived five hundred years because of your family. You're part of something huge."

"It's a blessing and a curse."

"Really?"

"Yes." He shifted on his chair, debating one more confidence and then decided it was long overdue. "For one thing, I like you. You see me as a normal person and we can have talks like this, where I get to be me. But I can't go out on a date with you because you're way younger than I am and the press would go nuts."

She studied his face for a second, then said, "Yeah. I of all people should know that."

"But I won't forget you. You helped me get over a very natural bump in the road in my life and I appreciate that."

She smiled.

The warmth of a genuine connection bubbled up in him, but the fact that he had to have a perfect life stomped it out, resurrecting the anger he'd felt the day he'd gone horseback riding.

Rowan was real, fun, honest. What he felt

for her was amazing. And he wasn't allowed to feel it?

Art Andino walked into Nevel's office and, glad for the interruption of those morose thoughts, Jozef rose. "Art?" he called to the man who was glancing around Nevel's work-space as if confused. "We're back here."

Art ambled into Jozef's office with a smile. When he saw Rowan, the smile became a scowl. "I'm sorry. I don't mean to interrupt anything."

Confused about why Art would scowl at someone *he'd* hired, Jozef said, "You're not interrupting. Rowan and I were just debrief-ing about yesterday's date."

He glanced at Rowan, then swung his gaze back to Jozef. "My sources tell me that the date bombed."

Ah, that's why he seemed upset with Rowan. "The date didn't bomb."

"Sources say you behaved more like busi-ness acquaintances than people on a date."

"We'd just met that day."

Art peered at Rowan again. Jozef frowned, as Art's gaze skimmed Rowan's haphazard hair and casual clothes. If Mrs. Jones had been the one sent by Castle Admin, she'd be offer-ing Rowan coffee and sharing pleasantries. Art peered at her as if she were gum on his shoe.

Because she dressed down? Because she was American?

Jozef wasn't sure, but he could see the disdain.

"Ms. Gray has done an admirable job of helping me get back into the public eye properly. You of all people shouldn't want me to behave like a starry-eyed simpleton over a woman."

Art's face soured even more.

Deciding to put the man out of his misery, Jozef said, "That's why I've chosen a plan for when I begin dating for real."

Art's gaze crawled back to Jozef. "Dating for real?"

Rowan shifted in her chair so she could speak directly to Art. "We agreed Jozef could pick his own dates after he went on three dates orchestrated by Sterling, Grant, Paris. Julianna Abrahams was a simple, happy date. Paula Mason was a more sophisticated date. I'll choose one more date." She glanced at Jozef and smiled. "Then he's on his own."

Art said, "I see."

"You and Mrs. Jones left the dining room before Rowan and her boss, Pete Sterling, laid all this out. But it makes sense."

"All this dating, Your Majesty…might not be good for your image."

He laughed and winked at Rowan. "I'm sorry, but the whole point of getting me back into the public eye was to keep me in the public eye. Ask Rowan, she'll tell you."

"If he goes back to being a hermit, your subjects will begin wondering about his health again. He needs to stay active."

Art peered at Rowan. She only smiled.

Castle Admin's employee faced Jozef, took a long, disapproving breath and bowed. "We'll talk again, Your Majesty."

He left the room and Rowan groaned. "Man, he's a grump."

"No. He's more like a stuffed shirt. Castle Admin is all about appearances and continuity."

"Continuity?"

"Yes. They work to keep things consistent from one reign to the next."

"I guess that makes sense."

"Every country must keep up with the times, but the world loves tradition and continuity. Castle Admin makes sure the subjects know that for all the ways the world changes there are other ways it stays the same."

"I saw that when looking around yesterday. I saw the castle is majestic and regal, but also historic."

His head tilted and he frowned. "Has anyone actually shown you around?"

"Not really."

"Why don't you let me give you a tour and then we can have lunch."

She shook her head. "I'm not so sure that's a good idea."

He thought she might have been concerned about Art, his horrible reaction to her, but she'd handled him easily. What they'd been discussing before Art arrived, however, wasn't as easily dismissed. "Because I mentioned that I liked you?"

She rose. "As much as I'm curious about the castle, it's my job to protect your reputation. If anyone sees you giving me a tour—"

"We'll remind them that you work for me and I'm showing you around, like a good employer."

"It will still spark rumors."

Being reminded that he couldn't even chat with a woman who interested him sent a bolt of frustration through him. He remembered the months before he and Annalise went to their parents to arrange a marriage for them. How he couldn't even glance at a girl in his class without rumors starting.

She turned to the door. "I'll see you next week."

She raced out, as she had the night he'd kissed her, and he came to a conclusion that froze his lungs, stopped his heart. He wasn't simply fighting his attraction to her. She was fighting her attraction to him, and it was probably stronger than she'd let on.

Crazy happiness flooded him. She liked him enough that she didn't want to risk spending time with him. It was oxymoron at its finest. He wasn't supposed to be happy that she liked him. It added a layer of complication he couldn't control.

And the kingdom wanted him in control.

The *world* wanted him in control.

But *he* wanted *her*.

CHAPTER SEVEN

RATHER THAN GO back to her rented apartment, Rowan drove to her office. Without Geoffrey at his desk, the small suite was eerily quiet. Preoccupied with her discussion with Jozef, she barely noticed as she strode inside the tiny space and plopped down on her desk chair.

After Jozef's unexpectedly honest comments that morning, she had serious second thoughts about sending him out with Princess Helaina. She pulled up her notes, all her research on the Princess, who'd been jilted by a cheating husband the year before and she studied them.

She understood Jozef well enough now to know that her original plan of him and Princess Helaina hitting it off, getting married and leaving the whole world grinning with pleasure wasn't going to happen. She'd nudged him into public life with two great women. His reaction had been to say goodbye to Julianna, happy to have met her, but not interested in continuing the relationship, and a more businesslike approach to Paula.

But he planned on continuing to date. He recognized he had to stay in the public eye. And if she was interpreting his discussion with Art Andino correctly, he wasn't looking at this as a time to fall in love. He simply wanted to keep his image intact.

Meaning, Princess Helaina might be the wrong woman to set him up with.

She sat back in her office chair, forcing herself to examine her conscience to make sure she wasn't simply thinking that because she couldn't stand the thought of him going out with a woman for real. Someone who would see him as a partner, a prospective mate.

He was commanding, powerful, sophisticated, sexy and funny. If to nobody but herself, she could easily admit she wanted him for herself. When he'd said he liked her and even admitted he'd thought about a date with her, her entire body had flushed with longing. She'd pictured them, with their walls down, laughing, having fun and rolling in twisted sheets, enjoying the electricity that always crackled between them.

But she couldn't have him.

He'd come right out and said it.

His position wouldn't allow it.

And she'd already had one guy publicly dump her. That was enough. She wasn't opening her heart again. Or even going out with someone who would cause a stir in the entire world when they stopped seeing each other.

That was why she'd declined lunch with him. The more time they spent together, the more she felt their click of attraction and remembered the spark of their first kiss. Only an idiot would blindly walk toward something she couldn't have.

Plus, she had to arrange one more date for him.

Princess Helaina seemed like the best candidate. First the movie star. Then the genius businesswoman. Now a royal. It made perfect sense.

But with Jozef indicating he would continue to date after the final date Rowan arranged—tossing himself into the dating pool like the world's most eligible bachelor—setting him up with Princess Helaina didn't feel right.

She rose from her seat and spun the laptop around so she could see it from the front of her desk, where she began pacing.

Princess Helaina was a starry-eyed dreamer. From the conversations Rowan had had with her, the thirty-something Princess *did* want a man to ride in on a white horse and save her. Her upbringing had made her something of a throwback, and needing a boost after her cheating husband, having someone rescue her seemed like a good idea.

If Rowan fixed her up with King Jozef and he treated her well, like the interesting, nice guy he was, Helaina would be smitten. Then, rather than have the happy ending the Princess longed for, she'd be sitting by the phone, waiting for a call that never came. The papers would undoubtedly make a bigger deal out of it than it needed to be. And her ex would read about it. It would be humiliating.

So, for Princess Helaina's sake, not Jozef's, Rowan would not make this date.

She walked to Geoffrey's office and prepared a cup of tea, pondering who she could get for Jozef's third date. She didn't let herself think beyond that, even though she recognized that his satisfactory outing with Paula Mason might result in him calling the software whiz when he began making his own dates. Which would be great for his image. And Paula's—

The thought upended her heart and suspended her breathing, but she shook her head and put her brain back on the task of coming up with a third date for the world's sexiest man alive—the guy she couldn't have.

Sipping her tea as she paced, she racked her brain, but no one came to mind. On her fiftieth turn from the window to pace back to the wall, she saw Art Andino standing in her doorway.

The shock of seeing him almost made her spill her tea. "Mr. Andino! What can I do for you?"

He stepped inside her office. "I need a moment with you."

She hadn't missed the way he'd been looking at her when he came into Jozef's office and found her chatting with the King. It was almost as if he could see or feel the attraction arching between her and Jozef.

If he was about to lecture her about falling for Prosperita's highest ranking royal, he could save his breath. She already knew nothing would happen there.

Heading for her side of the desk, she motioned to the chair in front of it. "Have a seat."

He gingerly stepped a little farther in the office. "I won't be long."

She placed her tea on her desk. "That's fine."

He sat on the edge of the chair and scowled. "I'm not exactly sure how to put this."

Oh, the damned fool was going to insult her. She stifled the urge to shake her head. She'd handled worse. "Just come right out and say it."

He opened his mouth to speak, but his gaze

landed on her laptop screen, turned toward him because she'd been staring at it as she paced.

"Is that Princess Helaina?"

"Yes."

"She's beautiful."

Rowan smiled at the softness that came to his voice. For all his crabbiness, there was a heart in his chest. "Yes. She is."

He looked up from the laptop. "Now, that's really a woman for Jozef. The American actress?" He made a disgusted face. "She was trite and simple. Paula Mason? There would be times when she would overshadow him." He pointed at the screen. "But Princess Helaina? Raised royal. Knows protocols. She'd be a dutiful wife."

"Jozef's not talking about getting married. He's just getting back in the dating pool. And he has to take his time. Do this right."

He caught her gaze again. "You were considering her, though, weren't you?"

"Yes."

He rose. "I want her to be the third date."

"Mr. Andino… Art…this could really backfire. Not for Jozef but for Princess Helaina. He's not looking for someone and he could hurt her. Which would embarrass her—*again*."

"You underestimate the power of tradition,

protocol and the comfort of being with someone who understands a life like his."

Not wanting to get into an argument, particularly since she'd already recognized that herself, Rowan said nothing.

"Do you think he isolated himself because he was being moody?" He snorted. "I've watched Jozef from the time he was a boy. I know what happened. Annalise has now been gone five years. His sons are raised. He knew it was time for him to remarry. He brooded at first because he truly loved Annalise. But I can see him coming to his senses."

Rowan frowned. "Coming to his senses?"

He tilted his head, studying her. "You think you're the only person who knows how to read people? When his sons came to me, I easily saw what was happening. I thought hiring you was only a way to wake him up. But you sent him on dates and got him ready to do what he needs to do—remarry. And a grateful nation thanks you."

"Jozef's not your puppet."

"No. But he knows how royalty works. Did he ever tell you the story of why he married Annalise?"

She shook her head.

"They were friends. They ran in the same circles. Both were expected to marry well and the pressure of that made dating miserable. Then one day, they had a conversation and realized they were each other's perfect mate. Not only did they like each other as friends, but each knew how royal life worked. So they made a deal. They would marry and have children and fulfill the responsibilities of their titles. They went to their parents and their parents arranged the marriage."

She scoffed at him. "You just said he loved her—"

"They came to love each other very much. But that wasn't a happy accident. That was two smart people knowing no one else in the world could understand the lives they were forced to live." He straightened in his chair. "I watched all that play out and I see the same signs now as when he and Annalise made their deal. He's lonely and wants someone in his life again, but he's wise enough to know he must choose from his own ilk, and he will."

He rose from his seat. "Set him up with Princess Helaina."

When Rowan didn't show up in the castle for three long days, Jozef knew something was wrong. She'd stayed away the week before his date with Paula Mason, the week after he'd kissed her. But this time he hadn't done anything to make her stay away. Yes, he'd admitted that he liked her but that had folded into normal conversation—

Or maybe not. She'd left the castle quickly, refusing the tour he offered her.

It killed him to think that he'd done something to offend her. He was on the verge of calling her to apologize when his computer pinged with an email.

It was late enough that he should have left it for morning, but when he reached to close his laptop and put it away, he saw the message was from Mrs. Jones and there was an attachment.

It was odd, but he was awaiting the arrangements for his third date from Rowan. If he'd offended her, she might have gone through channels to get in touch with him.

Angry with himself he clicked on the email, but there was nothing in it.

He frowned and glanced at the untitled attachment. Curiosity got the better of him and he opened it. Sure enough, the Sterling, Grant, Paris letterhead popped up. The missive was addressed to Montgomery Robertson, Head of Castle Administration.

Furious that she was arranging his third date through channels, he started reading. When he saw Princess Helaina's name, his frown deepened. As he read the entire text of the email, his blood began to boil and he called the livery.

The night duty driver answered. "Evening, Your Majesty. Is there somewhere you need to go tonight?"

"No. I want to use your car." He didn't often ask for one of the drivers' vehicles to get an opportunity to go out on his own, but this was important. Infuriating. Something he had to deal with.

"Sir, I brought my old, rusty SUV."

"That's even better. I'll meet you in the garage. Have it ready."

Tired from the day, Rowen ambled to her shower, stripped and stepped under the hot spray, where she stood for twenty minutes. She had the distinct feeling she would be fired in the morning. There'd be no question about her starting her own firm. It would be a necessity. She simply wouldn't get any overflow business or recommendations from Sterling, Grant, Paris.

She got out, dried off and spent twenty minutes drying her long, thick hair, before she stepped into silky pajamas—an indulgence she believed she needed to soothe her soul—and walked into her kitchen to make herself a martini—another appropriate indulgence given the circumstances.

Before she returned to her sofa to watch TV, there was a determined knock on her door. Frowning, she confirmed the late hour on the step tracker on her wrist and walked to the door. "Who is it?"

"Open the door, Rowan. I can't be standing in your hall out in the open like this."

Shocked that Jozef was in her building, she clicked the locks and opened the door. "What are you doing here?"

He stepped inside, closing the door behind him before he said, "I have never been prouder of anyone in my entire life."

Knowing exactly what he was talking about, she winced. "How much did you hear?"

"I got a secret copy of the email you sent to the head of Castle Admin from Mrs. Jones." He laughed heartily. "Not only did you report Art for telling you how to do your job, but also you refused to set me up with Princess Helaina."

"She is pretty." She winced again. "And a catch."

"And depressed. Her husband left her and goes frolicking on the Riviera with his new girlfriend and Princess Helaina's kids. He's been making her a laughingstock for a year."

"She needs someone to give her a boost."

"So, offer your services." He shook his head.

"I'll even pay for them. But setting the two of us up would have been a disaster."

"She's already a client. What you said is exactly how I interpreted the situation. Setting you two up would have been a disaster. But are *you* sure?"

"Am I sure of what?"

"That you and Princess Helaina wouldn't have hit it off?"

"Yes. I'm sure. Mostly because we want two different things."

"Really? Art was fairly certain the two of you could…you know… Make a match."

His eyes squinted. "Like get married?"

She squeezed her eyes shut. Then popped them open again to look Jozef in the eye when she made her confession. "Yes."

"Wow." He glanced around the room. "I think I need to sit."

He moved to the sofa and lowered himself to the cushion.

He looked so gobsmacked, Rowan sighed. "You can't be angry with him for that. He thinks you were isolating because you recognized that it was time to remarry, and it made you sad."

"I wasn't sad! I was moody because my sons are men. My job of raising them is done." He took a breath. "It was a perfectly normal reaction. I've heard people call it empty-nest syndrome. My children might still live in the castle, but they are adults now. I wasn't angling to get married."

The horrified way he said it made her laugh out loud, as she sat beside him on the sofa. "It is pretty funny now that you mention it."

"It is not funny."

She laughed all the harder. "Come on. Sure it is. Especially when you consider that it's grumpypants Art Andino picking your mate."

He snorted, then chuckled, then laughed with her. "Yeah. That's rich."

"Hey, maybe you were lucky. He could have chosen an old dowager."

He gave her the side eye. "That's actually what I thought you were going to do."

She gasped. "Really? You were expecting me to pick someone who wasn't suited to you?"

He shrugged. "Now that I know you, I realize you wouldn't do that. You have a great deal of integrity."

"Yeah, well, it might have cost me my job."

"I'd hire you."

She laughed. "Right."

"I would."

She glanced at him. "Then I'd be working full-time with a guy I was attracted to."

"I like that you're attracted to me."

She smiled.

He smiled.

"So you have a limo waiting outside?"

He winced. "I borrowed my driver's banged-up SUV."

Her eyes widened. "You drove?"

"I'm not helpless. Just pampered."

She laughed.

He leaned back on the sofa. "Driving here… *being here*...actually reminds me of when I was a kid, sneaking out, hanging out with all the wrong people."

"I'll bet you were a handful."

He shrugged. "The press was so bad when I was fourteen that I knew dating would be a nightmare."

"Is that why you struck a deal to marry yourself off at eighteen?"

He looked at her.

"Art spilled the beans. It's why he believed you would follow the pattern. Meet a suitable mate and get married again."

He groaned. "That guy's a real thorn in my side."

"You should fire him."

"I just might." He shook his head. "But I'll tell you this. I am scaling back Castle Admin. It's handy to have a bunch of people watching out for things like protocols and such. But they need to get out of my personal life."

She couldn't agree more. With that admission, she also realized her apartment felt different. Their interaction felt different. They weren't in the castle. There was no Castle Admin lurking behind a door. His kids wouldn't interrupt. No photographer would be aiming a high-powered lens at them. Not only had he sneaked out but also her drapes were drawn.

For the first time, they really were alone.

And she was in silky pajamas.

Confusion overwhelmed her for a second, but only a second. They might never have this kind of chance to enjoy each other's company again.

"Would you like a drink?"

She said it casually, not able to guess if he'd say yes or rise from the sofa and tell her it was time to leave. But she didn't want to miss this opportunity to have some real time with him.

CHAPTER EIGHT

He glanced at her martini glass then back at her. “I don’t think one drink would hurt.”

He didn’t know if he was talking about one drink impairing his ability to drive home or the alcohol content of one drink making them want to rip each other’s clothes off. Being alone with a woman he was ridiculously attracted to was so far out of the realm of his normal life that he didn’t have a clue. But he did know he liked being here.

He liked being totally alone with her. Where no one would criticize or critique him. He could be himself again.

And her pajamas might be silky, but they were covering.

She rose and made him a martini. “This is basically all I have. One bottle of gin. One bottle of vermouth.”

“Classic martini.”

She handed him the glass. “I’m not much for

sweet drinks. Don't offer me a chocolate martini or some fruity thing."

He laughed, wishing there would come a time he could offer her a drink. But he told himself not to waste the few minutes that he had by wishing for more.

They touched glasses then each took a sip.

"What else did you do today besides torment Castle Admin's most persnickety person?"

She laughed. "Not much. Now that I've sort of bowed out of being your matchmaker, I'll have time to help Axel the way I want to…unless I get fired when Pete goes into work tomorrow and reads that memo."

"I'll see to it that you don't."

She winced. "No. Don't do that."

"That's right. You want to start your own firm."

"Yes. But being fired isn't the optimal way to do it. Especially since I'd like to hang around and help Axel with his fundraiser."

He'd like for her to hang around and help Axel with his fundraiser too. That was three months away. He'd *love* for her to be in Prosperita for another three months.

"But I don't want you to go to bat for me. I can handle myself."

"I also like *that* about you." She was no helpless female. She was a star, who had worked for everything she had. There was something very sexy about that.

"It's kind of my trademark."

"I realized that." He swirled the liquid in his glass. "But you know what? That's about all I know about you. While you know one of the castle's best kept secrets. My wife and I were in an arranged marriage but technically we asked our parents to make the match, so everyone assumes we asked because we were in love." He met her gaze. "You know you have to keep that secret, right? Liam and Axel don't know."

She nodded.

And he knew she was as good as her word.

He also liked that about her, but they were getting dangerously close to him liking everything about a woman he barely knew. Maybe if she'd tell him something awful about herself, he'd feel better about not being able to date her.

"I'd love to know more about you."

She curled up on her side of the sofa, tucking her legs beneath her as she sipped her drink. "Well, I left my small town in West Virginia for New York City when I was twenty-two." She paused and the expression on her face said there was more to the story, but she smiled brightly and glossed over it. "I didn't have a job, didn't know anyone and ran through most of my savings the first few months I was there.

"But I got a job and found a roommate. Then the next thing I knew I was clicking with the work. My bosses took notice, and I was promoted and soon I was handling entire campaigns. Then Sterling, Grant, Paris recruited me for a job at their main office in Paris, and I thought, why not?"

That didn't sound good. "Why not?"

"Why not move to Europe."

"Oh." The excitement in her voice made him believe she wasn't running from something, as he might have assumed from that weird pause when she started her story. More than that, though, it was clear she loved what she did and had no regrets.

From personal experience he knew she was good at it. Still, he wanted to know more. Wanted to hear the little things that made her who she was.

"Did you have a dog when you were a kid?"

She laughed. "What?"

"A dog, a cat, a gopher named Skippy?"

"A gopher named Skippy?" She laughed heartily. "You know, Your Majesty, you have an odd sense of humor."

"It's easy to get an odd sense of humor when

half the known world is watching your every move."

"You have to laugh or you'll cry?"

"No. Nothing so serious. It's just plain weird."

And being with her, alone, in her apartment did not feel weird at all.

Which probably meant he should go before he started thinking this was okay.

He polished off his drink and stood up. "I must get Randal's car back to him."

"The rusty SUV?"

"That's the one."

She smiled. "I'm glad you came."

"I'm glad you shot Art Andino down when he wanted to do something incredibly stupid."

She grinned. "What can I say? I love my work."

He laughed and she walked him to the door. He stopped to grab the doorknob but the strongest urge to kiss her good-night overtook him and he turned to her. Before she could protest or even say good-night, he leaned in and brushed his lips against hers. She slid her hand to his shoulder and opened her mouth slightly so they could deepen the kiss.

He fell into it as if kissing her were as natural as breathing. He hadn't ever had an experience like this, and he couldn't believe he now missed it.

Craved it.

Really craved the heat and need tumbling through him.

He broke the kiss and looked into her eyes. "Thank you again, bravest, smartest person I know."

She snorted. "Let's not go overboard."

He turned, opened the door and left. Walking down the hall, he waited to hear her apartment door close, but he didn't hear it. He stepped into the stairwell, realizing she might have watched him leave and his heart lifted.

It was the craziest feeling to think about how much he liked her. Warm and fuzzy, but also thrumming with heart-pounding desire.

And wrong. He couldn't forget wrong.

Not wasting any time on the dark street, he raced to the rusty SUV. It was late, and the street was empty, but he didn't want to risk someone coming around a corner and seeing him.

He got behind the wheel, started the SUV and drove away, then he burst out laughing. He'd be lying if he didn't admit the risk of it was almost as much fun as seeing Rowan had been.

And seeing her had been amazing. No camera. No expectation. He had been himself.

Again.

* * *

The next day when he ran into her racing to Axel's office, late for a meeting, she stopped and said, "Good morning, Your Majesty."

"Good morning, Rowan. I'm guessing you're here to see Axel."

"Yes. Now that my work for you is done, Axel and I intend to make this year's festival the best ever."

He struggled not to stare into her eyes, as giddy happiness nearly overtook him. Having a secret, especially a secret relationship was fun—and he had to call it a relationship. They talked about real things. Truths he never spoke of with another person. She was a trusted confidante. Not just someone he desperately wanted to touch.

"I'm going that way too." He motioned toward the hall. "We can walk together."

They started down the hall. Feeling devilish, he said, "How was your night?"

She almost tripped over her own feet. "Excuse me?"

"Do anything interesting last night?"

She laughed. "I did have an unexpected visitor."

"Business or pleasure?"

She faced him. "Stop. Really." But her command was totally declawed by the laughter he saw in her eyes.

They reached Axel's office. He almost said, "I'll see you later," because it was the natural thing to say to someone when you parted company. But he wouldn't see her later. They no longer worked together. There was no reason for her to pop into his office.

Their secret relationship was over before it started.

That night, Rowan sat on her sofa and opened her laptop to review the long list of notes she and Axel had made in their protracted meeting. The kid might look like a slouch, but this project was his baby and he intended to do it right.

Evidenced by the myriad public relations tasks he'd found for Rowan.

She read them, categorized them by order, relevance and importance and then assigned deadlines.

A knock on her apartment door had her head jerking up. Setting her laptop on the sofa she called, "Who is it?"

"It's me."

Jozef.

She pressed her lips together to keep from laughing as she walked to the door. He stood in the hallway, dressed in the red and blue shirt he'd worn to the soccer game and holding a bottle of wine.

"I brought this. It's not a sweet fruity drink. It's one of the most expensive bottles in my collection."

"You collect wine?"

"It would be un-kingly if I didn't. I've made many connections by starting up a conversation about wine. Knowing wine, collecting special vintages is a badge of honor. You'd be surprised how many of your presidents stumble over something Europeans take for granted."

She chuckled and stepped aside so he could enter. "Is there something you need?"

"Actually, I liked last night's freedom so much I decided to repeat it."

She didn't know whether to be happy or proud of him. The more they talked casually, the more she liked it. But she had to watch herself with him. Now that his empty-nest syndrome had worked itself out, he could admit he was looking for something. Or maybe testing his newfound freedom. After last night's visit, it was clear he needed somewhere to go, and he knew where she lived.

She couldn't make anything more of it than that.

"Got the rusty SUV?"

"No. Orlando was working today. He drives a truck."

"A truck?"

"Beast of a thing. But that might have actually made my escape even better. No one is going to expect me behind the wheel of something that has mud flaps."

A laugh spilled out, as he confirmed her suspicions. "Ah. I get it. It's like sneaking off to a friend's house before your mom tells you to do the dishes."

"Do the dishes?"

"Wash the dishes."

He nodded, but he clearly didn't understand the unmitigated needs of an American teenager who always seemed to be confronted by a sink full of dishes that held her back from escaping to hang out with her friends.

She led him into the small kitchenette, where she retrieved glasses. "You don't know what fun is until you've spent your teen years plotting to get out of chores."

He poured wine into the glasses and handed one to her. "A toast. To escapes. I'm only now seeing how much fun they are."

She motioned to her sofa, a bit saddened that his attraction seemed to be all about his newfound freedom. He followed her into the cubbyhole that was the living room of her cramped rental apartment. She set her glass on the coffee table, then removed the laptop.

They sat.

"So..." She peeked over at him. "Change the world today?"

He thought about it, and she realized he'd taken the question seriously because the things he did really did change the world.

"There's a trade agreement that's hung up."

"Are you going to sweep in and kick somebody's ass for being slow?"

"No. The plan is to let them think they're winning until shipments from Prosperita stop." He leaned in. "Let's see how they do without tropical fruit."

She laughed and he sat back, getting comfortable. In her ugly sitting area.

Silence stretched out between them. Their ability to talk had fizzled into nothing, as he sat silently beside her.

Finally, he set his wine on the table. "I probably shouldn't have come here."

Disappointment rattled through her. Her attraction was alive and well. But his had been nothing but a longing to get out of the castle.

"It's fine."

"No. It's not. It's dangerous."

"You think someone's going to burst in and shoot us?"

He shook his head. "No. No one knows I'm here." He sucked in a breath. "It's dangerous because I want to do this." He slid his hand under her hair and pulled her to him for a long lingering kiss.

Happiness exploded inside her. He hadn't lost his attraction to her—

The movement of his mouth over hers blocked out anything but the desire that roared through her veins and caused her to glide her fingers through his thick, dark hair, as they both slid down on the couch.

His mouth devoured hers while his hands roamed her sides and her hands slipped from his shoulders to his hips, where they stopped suddenly.

"Don't stop."

Her breath stuttered. "I don't want to stop, but I—"

"Don't say it. Don't say you feel uncomfortable because I'm who I am. Damn it. Some nights I just want to be me."

The smidgen of anger that came through hit her right in the heart. She'd left her small town because being herself would have been living a Greek tragedy. She had the option of leaving, reinventing herself, creating a whole new life.

He didn't.

She pressed her palms to either side of his

face and pulled him to her for a hot, hungry kiss. She'd wanted to be with him from the day she'd met him. It wasn't merely foolish to pretend otherwise, it would hurt him.

"We could take this back to the bedroom."

He broke away, studied her face.

"You don't think you're sexy enough that most women want to sleep with you?"

"I don't want most women. I want you."

It was the sexiest thing anyone had ever said to her. Arousal pooled in her middle. Her breath became shaky.

She kissed him again until every muscle and joint tingled with need. Then he scooped her off the sofa and carried her to the bed.

They desperately undressed each other. When they were finally flesh to flesh, her breath fluttered out. His hands roamed from her chest to her belly button, followed by his warm mouth.

She wasn't about to let him have all the fun. A bump of the heel of her hand against his shoulder knocked him off-balance enough that she could tumble him to his back. Before he could react, she levered herself up so she could kiss him, and her hands could be the ones sliding along his muscular torso.

He only let her have control for a minute or two before reversing their positions again and soon they became like two eager puppies, wrestling for control with both of them winning.

When their hearts were racing and their skin tingled with need, he shifted them enough that he was on top of her. Looking into her eyes, he said, "You are beautiful. Too tempting to resist." Then he leaned in and kissed her again, as he joined them.

Her breath stuttered out as the amazing feeling of him filling her sent happy arousal careening through her.

CHAPTER NINE

TANGLED UP IN the softest sheets he'd ever felt with the most beautiful, sexiest woman he'd ever met curled against him, Jozef lifted the corner of the sheet. "I don't think these came with the apartment."

Pressed against his side, she laughed and snuggled closer. "No. I bring those wherever I go. When you travel as much as I do, it's good to have something that makes you feel at home."

He agreed, but too soon trepidation began stealing his joy. He'd gotten so caught up in her that he'd let his instincts run wild, and while it was undoubtedly the most intense, incredible sexual experience he'd ever had, it also tiptoed so close to being godawful wrong that he had absolutely no idea how to handle it.

"I haven't ever done anything like this."

"Sleep with someone you work with?"

"Sleep with someone I'm not married to."

She sat up, bringing the sheet with her to cover her soft, soft skin. “Are you telling me you’ve only ever slept with your wife?”

He laughed, his tension easing enough that happiness began bubbling through him. “You have to realize everything I did was under scrutiny. There wasn’t a place I could take a woman that wouldn’t be seen.”

“Wow.”

He heard the surprised confusion in her voice. He knew he was an anomaly to her, which meant she also had to realize how very, very attracted he was to her to risk so much to have her. Yet, their stations in life were so vastly different that he had no idea of their endgame.

He knew the biology of why he’d taken the risk. Anytime she was within two feet, his heart stuttered and his blood pounded through his veins.

But she was younger than he was. An American. An independent workingwoman who wouldn’t understand the restrictions of royal life.

She lay back down and traced her finger across his chest. “I think I’m honored.” She peeked at him. “You’re this great combination of intelligence and good looks that I just—” She shrugged. “I find it very sexy.”

Unable to resist temptation, he rolled himself to his side and flipped her onto her back again. "You do?"

She gave him a smile that sent a shaft of lightning through him. "Yes. I do."

To hell with logic. This did not feel like the time for it. It felt like the time to indulge, be decadent with a woman who felt the same things he did.

He kissed her deeply and this time made love slowly and thoroughly. He banished the flash of conscience that told him there would be consequences to this indulgence. He let himself plunge into the depths of her sweet warmth and turned off his brain.

But when they were both out of breath lying side by side on the pillows again, it switched on. Logical fear bubbled up. Not that she'd sell her story to the tabloids. She was too honorable to do that. But she was young. So young. And he had sons almost her age.

There really could be nothing between them.

"I've wanted to do that with you since the day I met you."

He closed his eyes and savored her words. That was what he'd liked about her the best. She'd never let him be King Jozef. He'd always been her client. A guy she was brutally honest with. Forcing him to be brutally honest with her.

And now here they were. Maybe only for this night.

This was not the time to change the way they behaved with each other.

He pushed himself up on his elbows. "I've wanted to do that since the day I met you too."

She laughed wickedly. "That means we're good. Stop overanalyzing."

"Is that what I'm doing?"

"I can almost hear the gears turning in your brain."

"Because I have responsibilities and obligations." He hated that reminding her of that was part of being honest. He took a breath, forced it out of his lungs in a long sigh. "If I were normal, I'd lay down, wrap myself around you and fall asleep until morning." He swung his legs over the side of the bed. "But I'm not normal. I rule a country."

She sat up. "I know."

He stepped into his pants. "Then you know I have to leave."

"Yes."

"And you're not offended?"

She had the good graces not to lie. "I don't know what I am. But I do realize the uniqueness of your circumstances. And if you're asking if I'm mad that you're leaving, the answer is no."

His shirt half-buttoned, he stared at her.

"I get it. Anything we have is going to be different. In fact, this night might be all we get. So, think it through, Jozef."

Her bluntness rendered him speechless.

"Before we do anything like this again, think through what you want. What we can have. What we can't. So we'll both know where we stand."

He left, jumped into the big truck and headed back to the castle, driving in through the servants' entrance.

He climbed the circular stairway for the first time in a long time not feeling alone or empty.

He knew their relationship was what he needed. He also knew their relationship was doomed.

So what did he want? What did he honestly believe they could have?

Rowan woke the next morning and stretched like a cat. Then she remembered why she was naked and unreasonably happy and she groaned. Had she really told a king he needed to think about what he wanted?

She had.

Well, that was who she was. Outspoken.

Maybe a tad too bold. After her ex, no one, not even a one-night stand would surprise her.

She strode to the shower acknowledging that given their circumstances, this could only be a one-night stand. Disappointment washed over her like the hot spray, but she focused on washing her hair and getting herself ready for work.

When she arrived, Geoffrey handed her a cup of coffee and shepherded her into her office to the video call with the Paris staff that had been already set up.

She took her seat and addressed the faces on her computer screen. "Good morning."

Everyone came to attention. A couple of years ago, she'd been dreaming of the day she'd command this much respect and have authority over the projects she was assigned. Today, she thought of Jozef and realized that, though she understood being the boss and having responsibility, it was only a fraction of the pressure he felt.

"Rowan?"

Geoffrey poked her, startling her back into the real world.

"I'm sorry. I zoned out for a minute."

They continued the call, with Rowan forcing her mind off Jozef and onto the conversations.

When they finally disconnected, Geoffrey said, "What's wrong with you today?"

"Nothing."

"Your cheeks are pink. There's a spring in your step. Did you go out last night? Maybe have a few too many drinks? That would explain the spring in your step and the loss of focus caused by a hangover."

She packed her files and notes into her briefcase. "No. I did not go out last night." But now that he'd mentioned it, she would have to be careful at the castle this afternoon. There wasn't any way she could change the color of her cheeks, but she could monitor the spring in her step.

She drove to the castle and walked through the front foyer and down the corridor, nervous, hoping she wouldn't giggle like a schoolgirl if she ran into Jozef. She wasn't concerned for herself. She didn't want to embarrass *him*.

She'd never given any thought to the real life of a king or how his girlfriends would have to comport themselves and, to be honest, that was more than disconcerting.

But she didn't run into him, and Axel awaited her with open arms. With his hair pulled back in a low ponytail, he rose as she entered his office.

"Good morning, best helper a prince ever had."

She laughed. "You don't have to be charming anymore. I already like you."

He chuckled as he motioned for her to join him at the conference table set up in the lefthand corner of his office. He became serious when they got down to the business of creating a few press release articles about the festival that Rowan would get strategically placed into magazines and high-profile newspapers like the *New York Times*.

He read her drafts, had a good bit of input based on his knowledge of past festivals and even improved her verbiage.

She sat back with a smile. "You're a natural at this."

"Luckily," he said with a cheeky grin. "It gives me a way to look official."

She laughed as his phone buzzed with a text.

"Go ahead. Check it." She rose and stretched her back, which appreciated the movement after hours of sitting. "It's time I packed up and got back to my office anyway."

"Don't tell me you'll be working into the night."

"I do have other projects I'm supervising long-distance. I'll go back to my office to find progress reports that I need to read before my video call with staff in the morning."

"A public relations person's work is never done."

She laughed. "You don't know the half of it."

He chuckled and glanced down at his phone. "It's Nevel. Dad's assistant."

"Oh." She nonchalantly picked up some files, hoping to disguise the weird thump of her heart when he mentioned his father. The incredibly sexy guy who'd come to her apartment and swept her off her feet.

That was a one-night stand.

The reminder served to get her attention back on Axel, but the warm syrupy feelings that floated through her when she merely thought about Jozef stayed.

"They want me in the office." He stowed his phone in his jeans pocket. "I'll see you tomorrow."

"Tomorrow's Saturday, but I can work." She slid the long strap of her briefcase onto her arm. "Technically, you get me every afternoon until you think you're ready for the festival, then I'll disappear as easily as I came."

Walking to the door, he said, "Thank you. I think your help taking the public relations end of this festival out to the world will change the event from local entertainment to a reason for tourists to come to Prosperita."

"That's good."

"It is. I want it to be the kind of tourist attraction that travelers plan trips around. Our country is small, but we're important. Some days I think no one understands how important my dad is."

She'd thought the same thing.

This time when she thought of Jozef, it wasn't a vision of kissing him. She saw that moment when he'd led Paula Mason into his conference room. When he'd caught her gaze and reminded her of who he was. A king. A world leader.

Her breath stumbled, but she was glad for the reminder. There were not two Jozef Sokels. One she could have and one she couldn't. He was one person. A king. And she needed to remember that.

Axel stepped into Jozef's office and he frowned. "Jeans?"

Jozef's second son fell to one of the chairs in front of his desk. "They are work clothes and I was working. Rowan came by so we could make plans for the festival."

Just thinking about Rowan being in the castle had Jozef's stomach falling to the floor. He'd sneaked out the night before, gone to the apartment of a beautiful woman and slept with her. Not that he believed sleeping with her was wrong. It had been the best thing he'd done in a long time.

But he'd sneaked out—

Had begun an affair.

With someone everyone in the castle knew.

When he should have been worried, the idea suddenly struck him as funny. He'd awakened feeling energized. His mood had been all sunbeams and silliness. Not very kingly, but he'd been feeling off center for so long that the lift had been—

Wonderful.

Axel broke into his thoughts. "So why are we here?"

"Your grandmother's birthday is in slightly less than two weeks. Your grandfather wants a ball."

"He wants the staff to put together a ball in slightly less than two weeks?"

"It's not like they haven't ever done it before. My father asks for very little. We will accommodate him."

Axel gasped. "You know who we should get to help?"

Liam frowned. Jozef almost groaned.

"Rowan."

Jozef recovered quickly. "She's not a party planner. She's a public relations person and a damn good one. We don't want to diminish what she does or make her feel like she's our personal property."

Axel whined, "All right."

"Castle Admin will take care of inviting all the right people, but you each get a few guests. The usual rules apply. Think through who you want to invite because Castle Admin will be vetting them."

Liam said, "Yes, Dad. I remember."

Axel slouched down in his chair. "You know who we should invite?"

"I said you could pick anyone you want. Just be aware they will be vetted—"

"Rowan."

Jozef fought the urge to squeeze his eyes shut.

"I like her. She makes everything fun."

Liam tilted his head. "I like her too." He raised his gaze to meet Jozef's. "I wouldn't mind if she were invited."

Jozef shook his head. "Let's not get carried away. If we invite her, we also have to invite her boss and probably four or five other higher-ups in her firm, so no one is insulted." He rose to indicate his sons were dismissed. "You know nothing is simple for us. We don't want to put Rowan in an odd position at her job."

Though she was quitting, no one knew that. Except him.

He knew one of her secrets. It both buoyed him and sent a feeling of responsibility through him.

Axel grinned. "Her bosses should thank her for getting them invited."

Liam agreed. "It's the perfect way to thank her for stepping in the way she did. You know, she fixed things without ever once making us feel like idiots."

Damn it. Jozef agreed.

He also knew if he protested too much his sons would wonder why.

CHAPTER TEN

ELEVEN O'CLOCK THAT NIGHT, Rowan answered a knock at her door and found Jozef in her hallway. This time he wore an old baseball cap and what looked to be his oldest jeans and a shirt that could have been a dust rag.

"You really don't want anyone to recognize you, do you?"

"Actually, *you* don't want anyone to recognize me. If the press discovered I was visiting you, they'd be all over you." He paused. "But you know that."

She led him into her small sitting area. "I do."

He casually sat beside her.

"So what's up?"

"My sons are insisting you be invited to a ball we're hosting for my mother's birthday in two weeks."

She knew his parents were still alive because she'd done her homework before she took this assignment. After a mild heart attack, his father had retired so Jozef could step up and take the throne. His mother would be turning seventy.

"That's right. She'll be seventy. I guess that warrants a party."

Even as she thought that, she remembered her dad's birthday party. The one she couldn't go to. She never returned to the place of her great humiliation.

But she suddenly wanted to. She missed her dad and her mom. And her brother and sister. She'd been gallivanting around the globe for eight years, perfectly happy. Why would she pick now to be homesick?

"My dad wants a party and Axel thinks we need to invite you to thank you for all you've done."

She brushed away the silly notion that she might be homesick and put herself back into the conversation. "There's no need to thank me. Especially for helping Axel. Not only is this a Sterling, Grant, Paris account for which you will be billed. But also, Axel is a very smart guy."

Jozef laughed. "He hides it well. Deliberately. His brother will be King, and as you know perceptions are everything for us. Liam must be seen as the smart, stable Prince."

"You think Axel's behavior is an act?"

"Oh, no. He's still a smartass, rebellious womanizer. He downplays his intelligence when Liam is around."

She laughed and struggled with the urge to kiss him. He was a king and she swore to herself she would never again forget that, but he was still a good dad.

A king. A sexy guy. A good dad.

She wasn't having trouble keeping his roles straight, but the more private talks they had the more sides she saw of him and the more she realized how much she liked him.

"Can I make you a martini?"

"You still have the gin?"

"Yes." She rose and walked to the kitchenette where she made two martinis. Handing him one, she sat beside him on the sofa. "Tell me about this ball. Do you want me to go?"

"I would love to have you there."

"Then why'd you feel the need to come and warn me I was being invited."

He glanced at his drink, glanced at her. "I thought it was a very good, very valid excuse to come and see you."

Her chest tightened. He had the most wonderful way of making her feel wanted. She supposed a sense of identity was the one thing she'd missed as she globe-trotted making other people feel special. It might also be the reason for her homesickness. In Convenience, she'd been an elementary school teacher. Everybody knew her. Everybody liked her. It was why her great humiliation had been so great.

"I thought about you all day." He shook his head. "I'm pretty sure I was also wearing a silly grin."

"My assistant told me my cheeks were pink and there was a spring in my step."

He laughed. Then sobered as he met her gaze. "Yesterday was nice."

"It was."

"I'm not sure of the protocol of one-night stands." He snickered. "I married young. I never got a chance to be a…player."

She laughed at the careful way he said, *player.*

"It's why the arrangement with Annalise made sense and why everything about you flummoxes me."

"I flummox you?"

"I only ever had these kinds of feelings for the woman I was married to. I've never been so hot for a stranger."

That made her laugh out loud. "Seriously?"

"I was just so proud of you for sticking by your guns and so impressed with your integrity in protecting Princess Helaina, and we had such a good time that night that I'd only come to your house to talk…but…" He shrugged. "I like you. The way you handled Princess Helaina was part of it."

"Thank you. You know I went through a whole crisis of conscience over it and had to very thoroughly consider why I was doing it."

"Really?"

She shook her head. "Of course! Jozef, the second I saw you my heart skipped a beat. I had to make sure I really was protecting her, not jumping on a convenient excuse, so I could keep you for myself."

He looked stunned by what she'd said and clearly couldn't find words to describe how he felt. "Are you telling me I'm irresistible?"

"No. If I'd had to, I would have resisted you…kept my distance." She looked at her hands, then back up at him. "I know nothing will come of this. We have an age difference, a class difference and two totally different career paths."

Brave suddenly, she slid her hands up his shoulders and clasped them at the back of his neck. "But we like each other. And working with Axel gives us three whole months, if we want them. If we don't make a big deal out of this, we can enjoy each other before I have to move on."

He put his hands on her waist. "You have to move on?"

"Starting my own company, remember?"

He leaned in, kissed her. "I remember. Your ambition is another of the things I like about you."

The kiss went on and on. His hands dropped to her waist and nudged her closer. She slid her arms to his shoulders again.

He unexpectedly broke the kiss. "I thought I was the one who was supposed to figure out what I wanted."

"You were."

"But you figured it all out for us."

She shrugged. "It's my job to think through personal situations. Your job is to keep the world safe and happy." She shrugged again. "But I think you would have realized we shouldn't miss this chance with each other."

"An affair sounds tawdry."

"You're using the wrong words. Let me give you the right PR spin. A match between us is impossible. But we like each other. So this space of time that we have is not tawdry. It's a gift."

He considered that. "I like your way of looking at things."

"So do I." She rose, gathering both of their martini glasses. "Let's not waste any time."

She put their glasses in the little dishwasher

and when she turned, he was standing behind her. He pulled her to him and kissed her, turning them so they were pointed in the direction of the small bedroom.

Kissing and unbuttoning buttons, they made their way down the hall. Almost at the bed, he yanked off his shirt and she got rid of her jeans. She fell to the mattress with a giggle and he joined her.

He didn't ask any more questions about how she felt. She'd been clear and she knew him well enough to see that he believed her. He trusted her.

As the shimmer of desire began to take her, another level of intimacy entered their relationship. *He trusted her.* With his secrets. With his heart, even if it was only temporarily.

And whether she understood it or not, she also trusted him. She hadn't trusted anyone since Cash. Not even her parents. No one really knew what she did. Oh, they knew her job description, but she'd never told them about the people she'd met or the scrapes out of which she had to yank them. She'd told herself she kept her clients' dalliances quiet to protect them.

But really, she simply had lost her faith in humanity. Kept herself on the sidelines. Said all the right things. Did all the right things. Without letting anyone close.

Now here she was, not merely naked and being caressed by a king. She trusted him.

The idea sent a shiver of fear through her. The last person she'd trusted—the last *man* she'd trusted had all but ruined her.

Still, as his hands found her breasts and their kiss became so hungry her breath stuttered, she knew she would not let this chance pass her by.

Though their parting would probably shatter her.

More than losing Cash had.

Rowan seemed overly bright the next day when she arrived at the castle for a four o'clock meeting with Axel. Jozef "just happened" to be in the foyer when she entered, only because he wanted to see her. The way he felt about her sometimes scared him, but he remembered she was as logical as a person could be. She hadn't forced him to see their relationship would end. She had eased him into realizing they had the gift of a few weeks together and they shouldn't waste it.

Wanting to see even a glimpse of her was part of the time he didn't want to waste.

"Good afternoon, Rowan."

She juggled her briefcase, purse and some loose files that she carried on her arm, clearly ready to work. "Good afternoon, Your Majesty."

"Here for a meeting with my son?"

"Yes. I believe we're briefing with your tourism board."

"On a Saturday?"

She shrugged. "I didn't have anything else to do. Seemed like a good time to fit it in."

"Well, the tourism board is made up of good people. They'll love you. Especially since you're helping them."

She laughed and he smiled. God help him, he could look at her all day.

But he knew he shouldn't. "I'll let you get to your meeting."

"Thank you, Your Majesty."

He turned to head up the stairs to his residence. When he reached the door, he paused. She'd be in her meeting at least two hours, which took them to six o'clock. What if he could get her to sneak up the back stairs and come to his home?

The idea appealed so much a ridiculous smile formed. There was something about seeing her among his things, in his bed, that made him outrageously happy.

He knew it was dangerous. Not that he worried someone would see her but that she'd leave memories all through his quarters, things he'd have to fight when she left—

He'd be fine. And he wanted to spend time

with her in his house. If he were clever, he could even have the kitchen prepare dinner for them.

He took out his phone and texted her.

What time do you think your meeting will end?

After only a few seconds, his phone pinged.

This might go to seven. Sorry.

No need to be sorry. I was thinking you should come to the residence after your meeting.

This response took a little longer. Not sure if she was busy and not able to text or if she was considering the ramifications of going to his apartment, he paced while he waited.

Finally, his phone pinged.

I'm not sure how sneaky I can be.

He decided her coming to his apartment was too risky.

Never mind. We'll do our usual. Except I'll bring food.

Another few minutes passed. He told himself not to pace but he couldn't help himself.

He'd been at her apartment three times that week. Maybe she wanted some time away from him?

His phone pinged.

No. I'll be up when the meeting is over.

Reading her response, he breathed a sigh of relief. Then he phoned the kitchen and asked for chicken and rice, a salad and wine. Knowing they'd send enough for two, he strolled to his office and worked until ten till seven. Right on time, his dinner arrived at his apartment. The kitchen worker set his place at the table in his dining room, and when he scurried away, Jozef retrieved another place setting from the butler's pantry and set a place for Rowan.

She arrived in his residence with a smile, and he pulled her to him and kissed her hard.

"Thank you for coming."

She dropped her briefcase, purse and files to one of the chairs in the sitting room. "A few times of you sneaking out of the castle might go unnoticed, but if we're going to do this for three months, we need a strategy."

Her use of the word *sneaking* reminded him he hadn't told her to come up the back stairs. Worry lit his nerve endings, but he knew she'd probably been careful, and she hadn't mentioned anyone seeing her, so he forgot it as he escorted her to the dining room.

It wasn't until they were sitting that he noticed the brightness of her cheeks and the dullness of her eyes.

She smiled as she inhaled their dinner. "This smells delicious."

"It's one of my favorites."

He took a bite of his salad, but she sat looking at the plate as if it were a foreign object.

"Are you okay?"

She shook her head as if to rouse herself. "Yes. I'm fine."

He could see she wasn't. He rose from his seat. "You are not fine. What's wrong?"

She closed her eyes and blew out a long breath. He didn't think she was going to say anything but she finally admitted, "I have a headache. I get them sometimes."

"I'm sorry. Had I known that I wouldn't have pushed for you to come here."

"It's fine."

"Is it a migraine?"

She winced. "No. Usually it's tension."

"So why don't we skip dinner and relax in the den?"

"No. You waited for me to eat. Plus, I should eat something."

He hesitated but sat again.

He picked up his fork. She reluctantly mimicked his move.

Hoping to take her mind off her headache, he said, "What did you do today?"

"Before my meeting with Axel?"

He nodded.

"I'm back on the case for Princess Helaina."

That surprised him. "You are?"

"Yes. Remember I told you she's a client? So far, we haven't been able to do anything substantial, but I finally got an idea. This time, I'm not thinking dates. I talked her out of trying to find another romance. Given that her husband is flaunting his relationship, especially when he has their children, I thought we'd go the other way."

"Other way?"

"We're setting it up so she can take her kids to a theme park, a private US beach and a few national parks. They are going to do a few weeks of healthy, normal, parent-kid stuff."

He laughed. "I get it. You're calling him out. Making him look sleazy."

"Sort of. The aim is more to make Helaina look like a good mom. But if we make her ex look sleazy, it's a perk. Her husband is scum."

"It's my understanding she was advised against marrying him."

Her gaze lifted and met his. "It was a love match?"

He saw a hundred things in her eyes. Mostly, a connection to them. To the myriad reasons they couldn't have a real relationship even though there was clearly something between them.

"Yes. It was a love match. Not all royals shy away from them. They do happen and they do work out…sometimes."

She said, "Hmm," then glanced at her food.

She hadn't taken as much as a taste, while he'd eaten several hearty bites. He set his fork down. "Come on. You look awful. Not even well enough to drive yourself home." He rose and pulled out her chair for her. "What do you say, you go lie down."

He knew she felt worse than she was letting on when she didn't argue. He walked her back to the hall and led her into his bedroom. She stepped inside and stopped. Her gaze lit on the picture of Annalise.

She faced him. "This is your room."

"Yes."

"Your Majesty…"

"Stop with that. I sleep in your room when I'm at your apartment. I'm not putting you in a guest room."

She didn't look strong enough to argue, so

he guided her to the bed, pulled her blouse over her head and ditched the cute skirt. Then he sat her down and removed her shoes.

She half laughed. "I feel like Cinderella."

"Don't worry. I'm not keeping your shoes."

She laughed again, but he pulled back the covers and lowered her to the pillow. "Try to sleep."

She nodded, her eyes closing immediately.

Worry flitted through him as he closed the door and returned to the dining room, but he told himself not to be silly. Or, worse, overprotective. Still, he didn't stop himself from checking up on her, his heart stumbling with fear every time he tucked the covers under her chin, and she didn't as much as flinch. Her shallow breathing alarmed him, but when she began tossing and turning, groaning as if she were in enormous pain, he couldn't stand by and do nothing.

He grabbed his phone and called his physician. When he realized it was Saturday night, he winced. "George, any chance you can make a house call tonight?"

"Of course, Your Majesty."

Without any further comment, the doctor disconnected the call and was at the door to Jozef's residence in fewer than fifteen minutes.

As he stepped inside the sitting room, he frowned. "You don't look sick."

"I'm not." He winced. "I'm counting on your discretion here."

George straightened as if insulted. "You do not even have to ask, Your Majesty."

He motioned for the doctor to follow him down the hall. "I had a friend who came to dinner tonight." He didn't stumble over the explanation. Technically, that was what had happened. "She told me she had a headache. But I could see in her eyes it was something more. She's been sleeping for four hours and doesn't seem any better."

They walked into the bedroom and Jozef tried not to flinch when George looked at her. With her bra straps visible above the blanket, George would know she was only wearing underwear. Still, she could have taken off her clothes herself.

That didn't explain why she was in his bed, not one of the five guest rooms. But he was a king. He didn't have to explain himself.

Using a scanning thermometer, George took her temperature. "Normal." He turned to Jozef. "Did you give her any over the counter pain relievers?"

"No. Should I have?"

"Maybe. But if she didn't take any pain

meds and doesn't have a fever, she might have a simple headache."

"She said she thought it might be a tension headache."

"Any history of migraines?"

"I asked her if it was a migraine and she said no. I'm guessing if she had a history of migraines, she would have mentioned it."

He nodded.

Rowan stirred. "Jozef?"

"I'm here," he said, jumping to attention when she woke. "Are you okay?"

"Yeah." She tried to sit up, saw George and yanked the covers to her neck again. She said, "What time is it?" but she looked at George suspiciously.

"Around midnight," Jozef said. "And this is George Montgomery. He's the royal physician. When you didn't move for hours, then started thrashing around, I worried that something was wrong."

George interrupted him. "*Is* there something wrong, Rowan?"

Rowan didn't hesitate. "I had very little sleep last night and a long day today."

"She's working with Axel," Jozef supplied.

"I just have a headache."

George nodded. "Are you feeling better now that you've slept?"

"Yes."

He snapped his bag closed. "Take some over the counter pain relievers and get some more sleep," he said and headed for the door. "You should be fine in the morning."

As the doctor left, Jozef hastily told Rowan, "Give me a minute and I'll get the pain relievers," then followed George out.

Walking to the entryway, George said, "I have a feeling anyone who works with Axel ends up with a headache."

Jozef laughed. "Axel's not that bad."

"No. He's not bad at all. But the kid's a go-getter. If he's in charge of the festival this year, he probably wants it perfect."

"He's trying to turn it into Prosperita's signature tourist event." Jozef grimaced. "And Rowan is our PR person."

"Okay. Mystery solved."

They reached the door. "I'm sorry to have bothered you, George."

"Jozef, after Annalise, I understand why you'd be jumpy."

"You don't think I overreacted?"

"Oh, you overreacted. But given your history, that's to be expected."

Jozef waited a second for a recrimination of some sort, but knew the doctor wouldn't interfere in his private business. It would be an insult to suggest he had to worry about his loyalty. "Good night, George."

"Good night, Your Majesty. And may I say one last thing?"

Jozef hesitated, but eventually he nodded.

"I understand you being jumpy about illnesses. But sometimes a horse is just a horse. Don't start looking for zebras in a world of horses."

Jozef laughed, George left and Jozef closed the door behind him. When he returned to his bedroom, Rowan was asleep again. He gathered pain relievers and a glass of water on the table beside her bed, then carried one of the chairs over from the reading nook and sat to simply watch her.

He hated that he'd panicked. But he knew why he had. Not because he worried she was sick in the way his wife had been, but because he liked Rowan a lot more than he'd let her believe. When they were together, he had the sense that she was *his*. She made him laugh, treated him as if he were just a guy, gave him a comfortable space of time and place where his world was soft and easy. Fun.

What guy wouldn't fight with the belief that she was *his*. What guy wouldn't like her—a lot more than he'd let himself believe if he would panic and call a doctor over a simple headache.

Still, they were reasonable about their relationship. When Axel's project was completed, she would leave, and he would let her.

And he would find himself in a black hole of loneliness again. This time it wouldn't be from a natural phase in his life. This time, he would long for everything they'd had together. His soul would mourn.

But that was his life, a succession of him doing the right thing. There could be no question he would do the right thing by her.

And that was to let her go.

She was younger than he was, on the cusp of her life. She deserved a real relationship where she could have kids, start her company and grow it to perfection, and go on vacation without a million camera lenses pointed at her.

He would be selfish to steal all that from her.

CHAPTER ELEVEN

SHE WOKE THE next morning in Jozef's bed. When she turned, she almost bumped into him. He lay on his side, leaning on his elbow, staring down at her.

"You look better today."

She stretched lazily. "I feel better." Then the full ramifications of what had happened rolled through her and she bounced up. "Oh, my God. I slept in a castle."

"It's not a big deal. I do it all the time."

He wanted her to laugh. She refused to. "I don't! And everybody knows that! My God! My car was in your visitor parking lot all night!"

Exceedingly calm, Jozef said, "No. It wasn't. I have coconspirators in the livery, remember? They drove it to your apartment."

She took a breath and fell to her pillow. "Are they going to sneak me out this morning?"

"Yes." He rolled to his other side and got out of bed. "But after a proper breakfast. You didn't eat supper last night." Wearing sweats, he pulled a T-shirt over his head. "And by the way, if you're feeling sick, you tell me that. You don't accept invitations as if you're afraid to say no."

She licked her lips. "I wasn't *afraid* to say no. I just couldn't figure out how to say no."

He sat on the bed. "When we're alone, there is no such thing as royalty. I'm just me." He smiled. "It's one of the things I like about you. I trust that I can be myself when I'm with you. When you accept an invitation that you should refuse, it's like you break that trust."

She nodded.

He rose. "Okay! You get a shower. I'll make sure breakfast has been delivered. We'll eat and I will show you a tunnel to the livery."

She laughed. "It's like I'm a spy."

He frowned as if he couldn't understand why that made her happy.

She shook her head. "Kidding!"

"Okay," he said, then headed out of the room.

In a weird kind of way, it was nice that he hadn't made a pass at her or even kissed her. Then she realized she hadn't brushed her teeth the night before and wouldn't be able to brush them now and she held back a groan.

She rolled out of bed and made her way to the bathroom but paused in the doorway. The room was enormous. The shower was the size of half of her entire apartment in Paris. Marble floors greeted her feet. Elaborate silver and gold tilework on the wall surrounded a claw-foot soaking tub. Windows didn't have blinds or curtains. Some had lightly beveled glass for privacy. Other windows were gorgeous stained glass. The light fixture above the double vanity looked like crystal.

Undoing her bra, she glanced around. The room was lush, luxurious.

Jozef had lived this way his entire life. Accustomed to opulence, he probably didn't even notice it anymore.

She stepped into the shower. Four butt-high jets hit her, as water poured from an overhead fixture that mimicked rain. The room even filled with the sounds of a gentle storm. If she closed her eyes, she could pretend she was caught in the rain in a forest.

She dried herself with the thickest, softest towel she had ever touched.

The hair dryer she used was powerful, yet somehow almost silent. A drawer in the vanity held four unused toothbrushes and tubes of various kinds of toothpaste. She stared at it for a few seconds, but she'd stayed in enough hotels to know the variety was meant to accommodate guests. She fought the jealousy that threatened to consume her. It was none of her business if he'd slept with anyone before her or would sleep with a million women after her. Though he'd said he hadn't, it was clear he planned to.

Turning off the little voice in her head, she took a toothbrush.

When she returned to the bedroom, she found a pair of sweatpants with an oversize sweatshirt and put those on to pad to the dining room.

As she entered, she sniffed the air. "Do I smell pancakes?"

He rose and pulled out a chair for her. "And waffles, French toast and eggs Benedict." He walked back to his seat. "I didn't know what you liked so I ordered them all."

She gaped at him. "Won't they think you have a guest? Or, worse, think you're crazy?"

He batted a hand. "No. Sometimes when I can't make up my mind, I ask them to send up this much food and the staff eats whatever I dismiss."

The way he said dismiss gave her a funny feeling. She'd just been in the biggest, prettiest bathroom she'd ever seen. A drawer in his vanity held enough kinds of toothpaste to please anyone—

She hated the crazy jealousy that rippled

through her again. Worse, she hated the feeling of being the world's biggest bumpkin. "Your life is so different than mine."

"Don't let it scare you." He pointed at the warming trays. "Pancake? Waffle? French toast? All of them?"

It didn't scare her, but it did focus her thoughts, remind her of who she was and who he was and how she didn't have a right to even think about, let alone care about how he would be having guests in his quarters after she went back to Paris.

She forced a smile. "I'm hungry enough that I could take all three. But I wouldn't be able to eat that much… I think I'll opt for the eggs benedict."

"Ah, this is all about the carb thing, right?" he asked, lifting the tray to dish out some eggs for her. "You look better."

"I feel a hundred times better. And I'm sorry I flaked out on you." As she said *flaked out* she almost groaned. She was with a cultured, well-spoken man, a *king*, and she sometimes said the most ridiculous things. She straightened in her chair. "It will not happen again."

He handed her dish to her. Gold trimmed and elegant, it winked at her.

"It better not. But I've already had my say

about you being honest with me. What's on your agenda for today?"

She hadn't missed how he'd changed the subject, but that didn't stop more questions from swirling in her head.

What did he see in her?

He didn't disrespect or dismiss her. He liked her. He liked being himself with her. But holy hell they were wrong for each other.

She turned her attention to her breakfast, so he couldn't see the questions in her eyes. "I have to go back to my apartment so I can dress for work and get my butt in gear."

"The drivers can sneak you out with a minimum of fuss. Your car's already home. Once we get some food in you, we'll call them."

She finally understood her confusion and dismay. When they flirted in his office or made out in her apartment, she was in familiar territory. Here, in his house, she was seeing how he really lived. Who he really was. It was breathtakingly awesome, even as it was godawful condemning.

She did not belong with this man.

Still, she reminded herself this wasn't permanent. She'd had affairs. There were men she'd been attracted to. With her mind firmly focused on her career and her heart not wanting another bruising, she'd found that to be a satisfying way of life.

Why was she worried that she didn't belong with Jozef? She did not want another relationship. Trying to have one was what got a person hurt. Knowing this would end was what would keep her from getting in too deep. She was smart enough to handle this.

She lifted her fork. "Maybe I could come back tonight, and we could finish what we started last night."

He caught her free hand, lifted it to his lips and kissed it. "I would love that."

Her heart melted. This was why she wanted him. It was lovely to have someone so romantic in her life. Even if it was only for three months. "This time we have to be a little more careful about the arrangements."

"I will alert the livery that your SUV will be in the visitor parking lot and tell them to make sure to take it to the garage once it gets dark. Then you can sneak down the tunnel that I'll show you this morning and slip out virtually unnoticed."

"Virtually?"

"You have to go through security."

It dawned on her that there were now a lot of people in on their secret affair. His drivers.

The kitchen probably suspected something was up. Now, security.

"Unless you want to spend the night?"

He smiled at her, and her heart did that funny thing where it felt like it melted and exploded at the same time, and she decided certain people knowing about them was fine. If Jozef trusted them, she trusted them.

It was all part of getting the chance to spend time with a guy who made her toes curl and her heart shimmy with joy.

This was as good as it got for her.

They ate and he dressed for the day in his dark trousers and white shirt. She made fun of him for being such a creature of habit, and he suggested that maybe she should help him pick out some clothes.

"Really?"

"Of course. They'd mostly be things I'd wear around the house or for football games, but you're right. It is a little silly to only have dress clothes for work and sweats for around the house. I should have more jeans, maybe some T-shirts."

She looped her arms around his neck. "Am I changing you?"

"I thought that's why Castle Admin brought you in."

She laughed. "They wanted me to get you out of the house, not change your wardrobe."

"We'll call that an added bonus."

He kissed her, then led her out the door. Instead of going straight, walking down the corridor that would take them to the circular stairway in the front entry, Jozef turned right. They went down a flight of stairs to another corridor that took them to a hidden door in a wall.

"This is clever."

He batted a hand. "This is overprotective security. We haven't had a threat in fifteen years."

They started down a long, well-lit corridor. "But you had one!" Curiosity overwhelmed her. "What was the threat?"

"Are you sure you want to hear this?"

"Yes! I love intrigue."

"This really was intrigue. Spy stuff. A gallery owner was arrested for selling state secrets."

Confused and a bit disappointed, she peeked at him. "A gallery owner?"

"We were never sure how he had access to the thumb drives containing documents he smuggled out behind paintings, but he was sending them out of our country."

"To?"

He shrugged. "Other galleries. Our security

people caught the crew on the receiving end, and though everybody went to jail, we didn't get the people behind it. Our gallery owner was as quiet as a mouse about his part in things through all his interrogations. He had a heart attack and died in prison before his trial. So we never did find out who was passing the information to him."

"And that was it?"

"Security monitored his family and friends, but his wife left the country with their daughter, and she did nothing even mildly suspicious. All indication is he acted alone. If he had co-conspirators, they fled or went underground."

"Okay. But that *incident* was kind of dull."

"It was a big deal to us and the country stealing the information on our defense systems. Believe me, we had to do some cleanup diplomacy." He chuckled. "But it was also one incident. We pride ourselves on being safe and quiet. A lot goes on behind the scenes to keep it that way."

She nodded. He stopped in front of another door. "The livery is right through here. This is as far as I go, though." He pulled her to him for a long, lingering kiss. "I'll see you tonight."

"Yeah, you will."

He laughed, then headed up the hall, but he

stopped suddenly and faced her again. "Might not hurt to bring an overnight bag."

His thoughtfulness made her smile, then she sucked in a breath and pushed on the door. As soon as she entered, one of the drivers snapped to attention, opening the back door of a limo.

No one questioned her. No one asked her name. No one even looked at her too long.

She headed to the limo and slid inside. Before the door closed, she heard one of the other drivers say, "Where's Axel? Wasn't he supposed to be here?"

All attention turned to the question of where Axel could be as the limo door closed and she almost felt forgotten…which was good. She was an employee, dressed in a too-big sweat suit, sneaking out of a castle. Let them focus on missing Axel!

That night, Jozef had dinner waiting for Rowan when she arrived twenty minutes early. She kissed him quickly. "It was the oddest thing. Axel canceled our meeting today."

He released her, inhaling her flowery scent. "It is Sunday. Maybe he decided to stop being a workaholic?"

"Maybe. But he didn't call. His assistant did."

"Oh, I'm sure he found some mischief to get

into." He led her to the dining room. "His attention span has been great for this project, but I'm not surprised he took a day to play hooky."

She laughed. "I guess I'm not either."

They ate dinner, then they teased each other back to the bedroom. She'd brought an overnight duffel bag, and he carried that and slid it into the bathroom as she fell to the bed. He joined her and they laughed and played until they'd driven each other to distraction.

When they lay, sated and happy, with her running her big toe up his leg, he took a long breath and once again wondered what would happen when she left. He knew he'd be lost. He suspected she would be too.

In his silent bedroom, he realized the only things he would remember about her were the work she'd done for him and their times together. Worse, when he'd asked her to tell him about herself, she'd kept the focus on her work. He knew nothing about her past, her social life. Then there was the matter of the pause in her story. The few seconds of hesitation as if she were debating telling him something.

She had a secret and though he had no intention of ever letting their relationship become public, normal curiosity nagged him to ask.

"You know… We haven't talked a lot about you. You told me things about your job. Even how much you loved moving to Paris. But really, I don't know any more than that."

She frowned. "I'm sort of married to my job. There's not much more to tell."

"I told you I got married young, didn't even date much before marrying Annalise. But you've played your love life very close to the vest."

She laughed as she ran her toe up his leg again. "Oh…you want to hear about my old boyfriends."

He wanted to know everything. An old boyfriend was as plausible of a reason for that pause as any. "Why not?"

"Because some of my dating past is…*embarrassing*."

Yep. There it was. The reason for her pause. "That's promising."

"I think you're hoping there's something bad in my past."

"No. I just sense you're not telling me everything."

"Are you afraid Castle Admin is going to investigate me and find something ugly…like I'm smuggling thumb drives out in paintings?"

She really wasn't one to give up information. Still, the more she hedged, the more curious he got. "No. You and I are just us. No one else involved, as they would usually be.

And I'm curious about the past of the woman I'm crazy about."

She sighed, clearly reluctant. "Okay. I was engaged to a guy and a week before our wedding he ran away with my best friend…the maid of honor for our wedding…and married her."

His mouth fell open as he tried to figure out how to react to that. Her fiancé and her best friend had betrayed her? It was no wonder she didn't want to talk about it. "That's…well, it's not something I expected."

"It was humiliating. In fact, when I think about it, I actually refer to it as my Great Humiliation."

She said it lightly, but he could feel an ever so slight stiffening of her muscles, as if the embarrassment of it hadn't quite worn off yet.

"I'm sorry."

She sat up. "Just stop right there. If you're saying you're sorry you asked, I get that. But I hope you are not pitying me. It's the one thing I can't handle. My God, I actually left town a few weeks after they made their announcement because the tension was so thick in Convenience, West Virginia. Small town…big gossip? It was a mess." She sighed heavily. "I now know it was the best thing that could have happened because I went to New York, got an assistant job at a PR firm and I was a natural fit." She snorted and levered herself higher up on her elbows. "If you think about it, it's kind of funny. I found my calling because somebody dumped me."

"Sounds more like destiny fixing a mistake than you being dumped."

"No. I was dumped. It was a great humiliation that I don't like to talk about." She paused then grinned at him. "Hint. Hint."

"Okay. I won't ask any more questions."

She said, "Good," and snuggled against him. "I should be leaving soon or I'm going to fall asleep. This bed is so damned comfortable."

She said it easily, conversationally, but he could still feel that fine stiffening of her muscles. He'd wanted to know more about her. But she didn't want to talk about it. And no wonder. He pictured her bright-eyed and eager to marry her fiancé and getting embarrassing, humiliating news. In front of her entire small town.

She wasn't as easygoing as she pretended to be. Seeing that, he worried that she might not be as casual about their relationship. More specifically, their upcoming breakup might not be as simple for her as she was pretending it would be. He'd experienced the ultimate loss when Annalise died, and he'd gotten through.

He knew that even though he would mourn the loss of what he had with Rowan, he would survive.

Rowan referred to her breakup as the great humiliation. And he understood why. Would their breakup hurt her as much?

"I can almost hear your brain churning over there."

He wanted to laugh to lighten the mood but couldn't. "Rowan, I don't want to hurt you."

"You won't."

"Really? Because I've already realized that I'll miss you when this is over. Are you telling me you won't miss me?"

"Of course, I will. But we're adults. We've both had losses. Our losses are different, but we know how to recover from the hurt of something we couldn't control."

"We could have resisted each other."

She laughed. "See? There's where you're wrong. We're like a magnet and steel. If we'd resisted, we'd have spent our lives wondering what might have been. This way we know."

"I suppose."

"Don't spoil it." Her voice went soft with desperation.

He understood that too. They didn't have forever. She didn't want him to ruin the moment with what-ifs. "I won't."

But protectiveness rose in him again. He would think long and hard about what they were doing. He'd be so careful that no one would ever know what had happened between them.

If it killed him, this would be their secret forever.

So she wouldn't go through another great humiliation if the press discovered their secret… or even Castle Admin.

CHAPTER TWELVE

THURSDAY EVENING, ROWAN and Pete rode up to the enormous gray stone castle in a limo for the birthday ball for Jozef's mother. A white-gloved man helped her out of the car, as another checked the authenticity of their invitation.

Waiting her turn in the entryway to the castle ballroom, on Pete Sterling's arm, she glanced beyond the receiving line into the enormous room filled with round tables boasting bright white linen tablecloths and centerpieces of yellow roses, Jozef's mom's favorite.

Axel, the first person in the official line, took her hand, as he looked at her strapless purple ball gown. "You look fabulous."

She laughed and introduced Pete and they moved on to Liam, but as they did, Jozef leaned forward just slightly and caught her gaze. He looked amazing in the red jacket with all the medals adorning a sash across his chest. Her heart stuttered. An intimate smile passed between them.

Liam caught her hand. "You're gorgeous, as always."

She thanked him, then laughed and introduced Pete. The next two steps took her to Jozef. Before Pete caught up to her, Jozef quietly said, "You're ravishing."

Their eyes locked and her breath stalled. "You're very dashing."

And suddenly Pete was right beside her.

Breaking their moment, Jozef said, "And you look lovely too."

Pete laughed. "I always wondered what people said in these lines."

"Now you know. We're as human as everyone else."

Pete nodded. "And you have an odd sense of humor, Your Majesty."

Relieved that Pete hadn't caught the intimacy between them, Rowan agreed.

Jozef turned to his left. "These are my parents. Their Royal Highnesses Alistair and Monique Sokol."

Both tall and elegant, the retired royals looked every inch the part. Alistair wore the same red jacket as Jozef. Monique was quietly elegant in a black lace gown, her salt-and-pepper hair swept up in a sophisticated chignon.

"Mom, Dad, these are Rowan Gray and Peter Sterling. They orchestrated my return to public life."

Jozef's father took her hand and kissed the knuckles. "Such a beautiful woman shouldn't have to work."

Monique rolled her eyes. "Don't listen to him. He thinks he's a charmer."

Rowan said, "Actually, he sounds just like Axel."

As Jozef's father shook Pete's hand, Monique leaned in and whispered, "It's where Axel gets it from."

She laughed. "His father can be fairly charming too."

Jozef's mom gave Rowan a curious once-over. "He can be. But Jozef typically reserves his charm for friends and family."

Rowan quickly said, "Working together we became friends."

The Queen said, "I see," but she continued to look at Rowan curiously.

With that, they were through the receiving line. A tall man in black trousers and a white dinner jacket asked to see their invitation again. He read it and motioned for a younger man in the same outfit to come over. The younger man led them to their table.

"They have a two-check system to make

sure there are no fake invitations," Pete whispered as they were ushered to a table toward the back. After their escort seated Rowan, Pete thanked him, and the young man bowed and scurried away.

Pete sat. "We're in the cheap seats."

"You didn't think we'd be up front, did you?"

"I don't know. You seem to be pretty chummy with the whole family."

"Not the parents. This is the first I've met them. Jozef tells me they live in Paris."

Pete gaped at her. "No kidding! Not even on their own island?"

Pete didn't seem concerned by her intimate knowledge of the family, but a sharp stab of fear hit her in the chest. After her slip with the former Queen, she should be on her toes. Instead, she'd casually told Pete something only royal insiders knew. She had to be more careful, or Pete would start putting two and two together.

Another twenty minutes passed as the guests filed in and were greeted by the royals. When they finally made their way to the long table that sat on risers in order that everyone could see the royal family, Jozef walked to the podium and lifted his champagne glass. What appeared to be two hundred waiters stepped forward and quickly poured champagne into the glasses of the guests.

"This is about as formal as we intend to get tonight."

Everyone laughed.

"A toast to my wonderful mother. A beautiful person inside and out. Happy birthday, Mother."

Everyone lifted their glasses and said, "Hear, hear." Everyone took a sip of champagne.

The Queen nodded happily and unexpectedly rose. Cleary confused, Jozef politely stepped back and gave her the podium.

"We'd agreed to no speeches tonight. We simply wanted to have a quiet party with family and friends."

Rowan glanced around at the four hundred guests as Pete mouthed, *A quiet party*?

"But now that we're here, I feel the need to say that I know I'm blessed."

An "aww" of appreciation rippled through the crowd.

"Our son has done an amazing job of leading our country and raising two sons. We could not be more proud of him and every day his sons amaze us. Our kingdom is in good hands."

Just like the day she saw Jozef going into the conference room with Paula Mason, Rowan once again saw his life, the importance of his life. This wasn't just a guy who was called "king" without any real say in government. He *was* Prosperita's government.

They ate a delicious meal, and as white-coated servers cleared the tables, the band played a song for the former King and Queen to dance in celebration of her birthday. Jozef danced with her next. Then Liam and Axel shared a song. Liam dancing with the Queen for the first half and handing his grandmother off to Axel for the second half.

Rowan sat mesmerized watching the royal family spread out and thank the crowd. She'd always believed American politicians bore a cross of a sort, having to reassure their constituents that they were the correct person for their elected positions. But a king, someone who gets his job by destiny, seemed to have a greater responsibility to prove he was the right person for the job.

Jozef did his duty well, but tonight Rowan saw the obligation of it. His only rest, his only reality was behind the closed doors of his residence—

Or, sometimes, behind the closed door of her rented apartment.

Pete pulled her out of her reverie. "Time to mingle."

She followed Pete into the crowd, the slit in the skirt of her purple gown allowing her to match his long strides. As Pete walked up to smaller groups and introduced himself, Rowan watched intently, knowing she'd have to schmooze with potential clients for her own company soon. But her gaze was frequently drawn to find Jozef. A tall man in a red jacket in a sea of black tuxedos was easy to spot. As Pete glad-handed, she watched Jozef move from group to group, pausing to dance with various women. Some older than he was, probably his mother's friends. Some younger. And some his own age, women who gazed at him with undisguised adoration.

Jealousy quivered through her. There were so many women who were better suited to him. And one day he would choose one of them. He wouldn't live alone forever. In fact, as Art Andino had suggested, his reclusiveness might have been the result of realizing he needed to get out but simply not wanting to acknowledge that his life had to move on. Now that she'd shown him the way, he'd find his new queen.

Maybe one of the women in attendance tonight.

The sadness of it nearly suffocated her, then Jozef walked up to her, but addressed Pete. "If you don't mind, Mr. Sterling, I'd like to thank Rowan for all her hard work by dancing with her."

She smiled at the silly expression that came to Pete's face. It took a few seconds before he realized that in a kingdom such as Prosperita, a dance with the King was an enormous honor.

Recovering as quickly as he could, Pete said, "Of course."

Holding her hand about shoulder height, like a gentleman, the way Rowan always pictured a prince would escort a princess, he led her to the dance floor. She saw the flashes of a camera and nearly froze.

"Relax. That's the royal photographer," he said, pulling her into a dance hold. "If this hits a paper, the angle will be that I gave you the privilege of dancing with me. Just as I told Pete."

"I probably should have curtsied or something, right?"

"No. You were fine. And you look exquisite."

A shimmer of longing whispered through her, but it was automatically tempered by reality. She was an export of Convenience, West Virginia. A woman with a bachelor's degree… nothing more special than that. And she was dancing with a king.

"I'm not sure about that. I only own one gown. This is it."

He pulled back. "One gown?"

"Take a close look at it. It might be purple, but it's dark and extremely simple. Most people wouldn't recognize it in a lineup. I'm a background person. Not someone who should be stealing the show. That's why I found this perfect, elegant, but not memorable dress."

He laughed. "Not memorable? Have you seen how sexy it is when your leg peeks out of that slit in the side?"

"Really? You think that's memorable?"

He twirled them around once. "You think it isn't?"

"Huh."

As she thought about that, his arm became restless on her back. "I feel like I should be allowed to pull you closer."

She looked up into his eyes. "I do too."

"But we can't."

"I know."

"You'd end up with more trouble than I would."

"I know that too."

Silence stretched between them. She half expected an apology. After all, it was his life that was hampering things. But he said nothing.

So she said nothing. What could she say? There was no answer for them except to accept their limited time together and realize they'd eventually move on.

"Tell me you'll meet me in my quarters later."

Her head tilted. "Later? Like after the ball?"

When he glanced at her, all the longing he felt was evident in his dark, brooding eyes. "Yes."

How could a woman resist those eyes?

"I'll have to ditch Pete. We came together."

He laughed. Simple and pure, it enveloped them in their own private world. "I could have him arrested."

"He liked your sense of humor, Jozef, but I don't think he'd get the joke in that."

"Too bad." He paused. "Can you get away?"

His soft, serious voice trembled over her nerve endings, promising things she loved, things she was coming to need. Their strong connection filled her soul, called to her body, and there wasn't a single piece of her DNA that could have refused him.

"There's always a way if you're committed to finding it."

"Then you'll meet me?"

Crazy wonderful feelings rolled through her. She'd never felt this way with or about anyone before. Not even Cash.

The realization nearly stopped her cold. She hadn't thought about her ex-fiancé in years, except with distaste. But tonight, she could remember their good times, remember why she'd loved him and feel nothing. No sense of loss. No humiliation.

Jozef had made her feel lovable again. Normal. Like a woman, not a woman scorned.

"I'll meet you."

Two hours later, though, she hadn't managed to sufficiently ditch Pete.

Standing with him in a foyer full of people who were talking, saying goodbyes, waiting for their names to be called for their limos, she racked her brain for an answer.

When inspiration finally struck, she faced Pete. "You know, I think I forgot something in Axel's office. I should go back and get it. You take the limo and head home. I'll call a cab."

"Nonsense," Pete said. "I'll walk to Axel's office with you. We can get what you forgot and be back in time to get our limo."

Axel suddenly appeared at her side. "Thank you again, Rowan, for your help." He glanced at Pete then back at her. "But there are a few ideas I've had about our project. If you had a moment, we could discuss them."

She looked at him. He nudged his head toward Pete, as if he knew she was trying to ditch him.

"I could take a minute with you, Axel."

"Good." He faced Pete. "No need to worry. I'll have one of our limos take her home."

Pete smiled, as their limo was called. "I guess I'll see you in the morning then."

She nodded and he scurried off.

She pivoted to face Axel. "What are you doing?"

"Rescuing you." He turned to walk away but spun around again. "Don't take these stairs. There's another set. Make the first right, then two lefts. They're pretty deep into the castle, but you'll find them." He pointed down a corridor to his left, then he grinned. "And don't worry, we'll never speak of this."

With that, he ambled into the crowd, thanking guests, making everyone laugh.

Seizing her moment, she slid out of the press of people waiting for limos and down the deserted hall and two more hallways that were so deserted the lights had been dimmed. Then she found the other stairway. Lifting her skirt, she raced up the steps.

Walking down the hall to Jozef's quarters, she wondered how the hell she'd get inside his apartment. She envisioned herself waiting in the hall, as she had the day he'd had his miniscule version of a meltdown, but as she approached the door, it opened.

Jozef pulled her inside, closed the door and pressed a long, lingering kiss to her mouth.

"I've wanted to do that all night."

"So have I."

This man had freed her from her demons.

Cash had damaged something in her soul. Jozef had fixed it. The monumental realization almost rendered her speechless. She should tell him. But the conclusion that was the most important thing to happen in her life in a decade really wasn't relevant to his life.

His jacket removed and his tie loosened, he motioned toward his sitting room. "Drink?"

"I think I maxed out on champagne." As she spoke, he poured himself a glass of bourbon and she realized she hadn't seen him with a drink in his hand at the ball, except the glass of champagne when he'd made his toast.

He sat on the sofa, and, still in her gown, she sashayed over and sat beside him.

"This is nice."

The quiet of the castle settled around them. She nestled into his side. She was so confused and appreciative that someone had finally gotten her beyond her great humiliation, that she almost felt she was having an out-of-body experience. In a kind world, she'd ride off in the sunset with the man who'd freed her.

But that couldn't happen. A sense of injustice poured through her like icy water. How could she have to walk away from someone she loved so much?

The casual thought froze her.

Dear God. She loved him.

Gazing into his eyes, she realized she couldn't tell him that her feelings had exploded, and her heart vibrated with longing that would go unfulfilled. She could see herself spending the rest of her life with him—if he weren't a king.

But he was a king.

She swallowed hard.

"What did you think of your first royal ball?"

She said, "Amazing," but the ache in her heart swelled until it grew so big she felt empty, hollow. Jozef had changed her life, but she couldn't admit that to anyone. She couldn't be publicly proud of him. She couldn't tell anyone they were in a relationship. Because they couldn't be in a real relationship. The press would poke into her past and then eat her alive when they found Cash. She might be beyond her great humiliation, but it would be fresh meat to them. The way to embarrass this wonderful, thoughtful, hardworking king would be through her.

She supposed accepting that was how she thanked him for bringing her back to life.

"A ball that took an entire castle staff two weeks to organize was just amazing?"

Forcing herself beyond the feelings shredding her, she faked a laugh and twisted so she could face him. "*Amazing* is a big word in my vocabulary." She waited a second, then she said, "Did *you* enjoy *yourself*?"

"My mother had a wonderful time. That's what we were aiming for."

She realized again how orchestrated and goal-oriented everything in his life was.

Except them. Their secret relationship might be the only part of his world that was unscripted and genuine.

Accepting that, accepting her place in his life took deeper meaning.

She was his respite. Being with her was the one time he was himself. Something he needed. If she could protect that with secrecy, then so be it.

He finished his bourbon and she reached for the zipper in the back of her dress. With a slow, steady swish, she lowered it. When she rose, the gown puddled at her feet. His eyebrows rose as she stepped out of it, but his eyes sharpened with need when—in nothing but purple bra and panties—she put her knees on either side of his thighs.

"What do we have here?"

"A little seduction because while everybody else was having fun, you were working."

He slid his hands to her bottom. "It's the job."

She leaned in, kissed him, then pulled back.

"In some ways, I think being King is the opposite of a normal job. The hardest part of your position is when you're not supposed to be working, because that's your most important work. Schmoozing. Reassuring people. Making deals when people are comfortable and don't realize you are guiding them to see things your way."

"You're very observant."

She kissed him again. "And that's *my* job." It was also what she owed him for helping her get beyond Cash's betrayal. Reassurance. Security. Secrecy.

She undid her bra. Let it fall to his lap.

Their gazes met as his hands moved from her bottom to her breasts. She leaned in and kissed him. Sadness that this wouldn't last rippled through her, but she fought it. From here on out, every day, every hour, every minute they had together was precious.

His hands skimmed her back as their kiss became steamy. Her fingers inched to the buttons of his shirt, opening them so she could remove his shirt and touch him.

When things heated to a boiling point, he rose from the sofa, taking her with him and carrying her to his bed.

With his breath coming in irregular pants, Jozef rolled to his side and fell to his pillow.

"You are amazing."

She levered herself up on her elbows. "I think we are an amazing team. You know how some people are just made to do what they do? Well, we're made to do that."

He laughed.

Beautifully pink and perfect in her nakedness, she turned on her side so their eyes could meet. "I know we've never really talked about this, but I'm sort of glad we aren't public with our relationship."

His chest tightened and disappointment flooded him, though he knew it shouldn't. They'd made the deal that their relationship would be temporary. The secrecy part was a natural spin-off of that.

"Watching you tonight, I realized that if anybody knew we were in a relationship, the press would dig so far into my past they'd find my great humiliation."

Though he knew her great humiliation had been awful for her, he now understood that she referred to it so condescendingly to diminish its power over her. Then the strangest thought hit him.

"You do realize you PR'd yourself."

"What?"

"You belittle your past by giving it a cute handle. Your great humiliation. But you could actually use your past to explain why you're such a good PR person."

"Really? You don't think that finding a way to explain my past to *your* media is wishful thinking."

Confused, he glanced at her. "That's what you got from that? That I was looking for a way to explain *your* past to *my* press?"

"I don't know. I've rolled some of this around in my head lately, and I'm just glad we aren't giving them a chance to embarrass you through me."

"That's because you always think like a PR person. My PR person. You're protecting me."

She laughed and dropped to her pillow again. "That's me. Always working."

He had been tired from the long day but being with her refreshed him. Obviously, it also relaxed him to the point that he didn't think about what he said. Because talking about her job had somehow taken them perilously close to talking about the future. And they had none.

Those odd feelings galloped through him again. Acknowledgment that what they had wasn't permanent did not make him happy—didn't relieve his mind—the way it should. This was simply supposed to be an affair. A once-in-a-lifetime romance that would revitalize their damaged souls, but end. He wasn't supposed to let his thoughts veer toward a future that could never be.

Mostly because being with him for real would change her life in ways no one should have to accommodate.

Telling himself he was thinking too hard, too much, and that wasn't what their relationship was about, he reached for her again, pulled her to him and bit her neck.

She laughed and he suddenly realized that they played like happy innocents when they made love. There were no rules and there was no one watching, no one who cared. No one who even *knew*.

Because that was the way it had to be.

As a king, he understood that.

Now he knew she did too.

Maybe that was what her comment had been about? Her way of reassuring him that she truly understood their limits. Though, technically, she was the one who had established their limits, when she'd told him what they had would be temporary.

Strange feelings stuttered through him again.

Everything that had once reassured him suddenly angered him.

He fought back the anger, and they made love in the unreserved, fun way that defined their feelings for each other, then drifted off to sleep like two people without a care in the world.

The next morning, Jozef awoke with her in his bed. He fumbled for his phone to see the time. But hoping for it to be before dawn was only kidding himself. Light wasn't pouring in through the thick drapes, but there was a peek of it. One slim beam of condemnation.

With his parents in town, he had a breakfast obligation. Plus, the former King and Queen had free run of the castle. His dad could be in the livery. Or roaming the halls reminiscing. But he hadn't thought about breakfast or his roaming father, the night before. He'd been content having Rowan at his side and had fallen asleep like a man who didn't have a care in the world…or responsibilities.

Recognizing the gravity of this kind of slip, he bounced up. He reached over to wake her, but he stopped. Her abundant red hair lay on the pillow and cascaded to her breasts. The world was silent and she was perfection. Having her there when he woke up filled him with something he could neither define nor describe.

And whether he wanted to admit it or not, what he'd felt the night before as he tried to sort everything out was anger, mixed with sorrow that they couldn't think of the future.

Pressing his lips together to ward off emotions he didn't want and wasn't allowed to have, he tapped her shoulders. "Rowan. You have to get up."

Her eyelids lifted slowly, and he could see the very second she realized they'd spent the entire night together. They'd done it before, so it took another second for her to think it through.

Her green eyes widened in horror. "Oh, my gosh! I'm so sorry! Your parents are here. Everybody's probably in the dining room, waiting for you."

"It's not a big deal. We've handled this before," he said, sliding out of bed and into the trousers of his formalwear.

She rolled out of bed and glanced around as if confused before she winced. "My clothes are in your sitting room."

"Don't you have something in your overnight bag?"

She sighed. "No. I just have clean undies, a toothbrush, my own shampoo, that kind of stuff."

Before he could offer to get her things, she raced out of the bedroom. By the time he made it up the hall, she was fully dressed in her purple gown. She ran to the door, but he caught her hand before she could leave.

Half of him wanted to laugh at the silliness

of their situation. The other half recognized this as part of who they were. Two people who weren't allowed to be together.

They looked into each other's eyes. Recognition passed between them. *They weren't allowed to be together.*

"You think your drivers will be expecting me?"

"Maybe," he said, forcing himself to dismiss dismal thoughts that they had no future. "But my parents have access to the tunnels, the private elevators and stairways. It's not a good idea for you to be walking in any of them. Get yourself to the front entrance, and I'll call downstairs and have a car waiting for you."

Lightening the mood, she said, "The rusty SUV?"

"Or maybe the truck with the mud flaps."

She laughed, as he wanted her to, so he kissed her. He kissed her because kissing her was the best feeling in the world, but also because she didn't criticize or call him out about their need for secrecy, for as much as an outsider could understand the rules and restrictions of his world, she understood.

CHAPTER THIRTEEN

ROWAN SNEAKED DOWN the stairs and out of the castle. As if my magic, there was a limo. Laughing, she shook her head as the driver opened the back door.

She gave him her address and he drove her home—not to her office, though it was close to her start time. She might have had to sneak out of the castle in her gown, but she wouldn't wear it to work.

Because she arrived at the office late, Geoffrey met her at the door with a cup of coffee and that day's messages, added to his insatiable curiosity about the ball. She answered his questions as if she'd been nothing more than a lucky PR person who'd gotten a royal invitation and he'd seemed to accept that.

"Now that the King's mother's birthday celebration is over, we can't forget about tonight's gallery opening."

Her eyes widened.

"Oh, please. Do not tell me you forgot."

"I didn't." Because they'd ditched the idea of a third date, she'd scheduled Jozef to go to a gallery opening with his sons to keep him in the public eye. The birthday ball for his mother had overshadowed it, but the three Zokol men were to go to the gallery an hour before the official opening, so they could have the place to themselves, and then slip out to have a late dinner together.

This was not a big deal. Now that Geoffrey had reminded her, she was on top of it.

"After the protocols and security that I saw at that ball last night, a gallery opening should be a piece of cake."

"A nice way to get him out in public."

"Yes. Without a date," she said, keeping up the conversation as she strode to her desk. "It will be good to have him go out on his own. Now that he's been out, he can keep going out. And when he decides to find his own dates, they will be his to plan."

Geoffrey drew in a satisfied breath. "And his world is saved."

She laughed, but the knife twisted in her chest again. She might have been guiding him to this point, but the part of her that loved him did not like it.

She and Geoffrey spent some time working on Axel's fundraiser. He suggested they go to lunch together, but she declined. The realizations she'd had the night before, that she'd fallen in love with the guy who had all but erased her great humiliation, added to the reminder that they had no future, had soured her stomach. She needed time to—as Jozef said—PR herself. Remind herself why the life she'd been building was enough and focus on her own future.

And her future was her own company. A solid reputation. Which meant no one could find out about her and Jozef. She also couldn't mourn not having a future with him. She had to work.

Her mind fixed and Geoffrey out of the office, she investigated office space in Manhattan, thought about how much staff she would need, if any, when she opened her doors. Pondered hiring Geoffrey away from Sterling, Grant, Paris.

An hour later Geoffrey was back with a sandwich for her.

But she didn't stop working. Remembering Axel's vision of turning their charity fundraiser into something that would ultimately become a tourist destination, she mulled ideas until she thought of an angle.

She ran it by Geoffrey, who suggested they

video conference with their Paris team, looking for problems, and before she knew it, it was five o'clock.

A knock on the door of the outer office had both of their heads snapping up.

"Delivery. Somebody has to sign for it."

Geoffrey waved her back down when she rose. "I'll sign."

Tired, she stretched in her desk chair.

Geoffrey returned to her office carrying a big box that looked more like a gift than a document.

"What's that?"

He shrugged. "I don't know. Why don't you open it? It's addressed to you."

The box was so big she had to stand up to slide the big red, ribbon off. She lifted the lid to find red tissue paper and a card.

Geoffrey's eyes grew huge. "What is it? Do you have a secret admirer?"

She laughed. "It's from the King."

His eyes grew even bigger.

"Remember the time I forced him to wear the red and blue striped polo shirt?"

He frowned but nodded. "Well, he wants me to wear this tonight."

"You're going to the gallery opening?"

"Apparently, he thinks I am. I did show up at his date with Julianna Abrahams. And I was in the foyer when he met Paula Mason." She let her voice drift away. "He probably does think I'll be going tonight."

Geoffrey reached for the box. "In this…" He pulled out an exquisite white gown dusted with tiny multi-colored flowers and whistled. "Wow." He nudged the dress to her. "Feel how soft this material is!"

The dress was long and sleek, silky and sexy—yet an innocent white with delicate flowers.

She swallowed and slid the card to her desk. She'd read Geoffrey a simpler version of what Jozef had said, not mentioning the part about her escaping the castle that morning in the purple gown. Or the part telling her that she was beautiful and wonderful and deserved to be noticed.

"You'd better get going. Remember, the royals go into the gallery alone an hour earlier than the invited guests."

"Okay, I remember. I'll leave now."

But when she lifted the box from her desk, she knocked the card to the floor. Geoffrey bent to pick it up. His gaze rose to hers. "There's a lot more in this card than what you told me."

She licked her lips. "Yeah."

"What's going on?"

She cleared her throat. "I always wear the purple gown, everywhere I go and last night he noticed."

"At the ball?"

She winced because she didn't want to lie. "I told him I always wear the simple gown, so I won't be noticed and sending this dress is his way of teasing me."

Geoffrey glanced down at the card again before he handed it to her, probably seeing that part about her sneaking out of the castle in the purple gown that morning. But as a faithful employee, he said, "Sure. I get it."

She sucked in a breath. "Don't make a big deal out of this. He's fifteen years older than I am, has sons closer to my age than his, and he's a king. Even if we wanted to pursue all our teasing and flirting, we couldn't."

He glanced at the card in her hands. "Sounds like you've been doing more than teasing and flirting."

"But that's all it can be."

"You're sure?"

"Yes! You know what will happen if he starts to date me. My secrets will come out."

He frowned. "*Your* secrets?"

She'd never told Geoffrey—or anyone she worked with—her story, but she could see he needed answers, and if she wanted him to keep her secret about Jozef, she had to fully take him into her confidence.

She fell to her desk chair. "I was engaged. A week before my wedding my fiancé came to my house with my best friend to tell me they'd run away and gotten married."

Geoffrey's eyes widened. "Oh, honey."

"It was ugly. I left town. But look around you. I made a great life. Unfortunately, I don't think the press will home in on the good I've done. Just my great humiliation. I wouldn't care if they dragged me through the mud, but they'd do a number on Jozef and I can't let that happen."

Geoffrey nodded. "Sure. Makes sense."

"Plus, Jozef also lost his wife, Annalise. If I'm understanding his situation correctly, she was the perfect spouse for him. If he replaces her, it will be with someone like her. He doesn't believe in romantic love, and I respect that."

Geoffrey sighed and shook his head. "Oh, honey. You're already in love."

She wanted to deny it but couldn't. She'd realized it the night before. "It's okay. I've lost at love before, remember? I don't belong with a king. And he doesn't really want me."

"He doesn't want you?" Geoffrey's face scrunched in confusion. "How do you know?"

"We sort of made a deal that this would only be temporary. I understood sneaking around in the beginning. When everything was just about fun and spending time together, I didn't need to dig any deeper. But yesterday, at the ball—" She shrugged. "I could just see that I don't fit in his world and he's known it all along."

"Or—maybe he doesn't know how to bring your relationship into the public eye. After all, you're the woman who was finding him dates last month."

She tried to laugh but it came out hollow. "You're missing what I'm telling you. He's a king through and through. A guy who knows he has to do what his country needs him to do. Meaning, if he marries, it will be to someone more suited than I am. Think about it. I was the woman finding him dates. Now I'm the woman helping him come out of his shell. I think I'm his rebound relationship. Not the woman he'll fall in love with. The woman he walks away from to find real love."

Saying it out loud made her voice quiver with pain.

Geoffrey opened his arms to hug her. "Come here."

She took a step back. "I can't stand pity. It's why I left West Virginia. I don't want to be pitied. I want to be strong. *Never hurt*. Independent."

Geoffrey said, "And alone?"

"Maybe." She shook her head. "It doesn't matter. Being independent and strong and helping Jozef are more important." But in her heart, she suddenly realized that if Jozef would ask to take their relationship public, she'd risk it.

But he wouldn't. She knew he wouldn't. Because she was his rebound relationship.

It fell into place so clearly in her head that she almost couldn't believe she'd been so stupid that she didn't see it before this.

She drove her tired SUV back to her apartment, then clamored up the steps, wrestling with the big dress box, debating whether she should go to the gallery opening. Having everything about their relationship fall into place hurt so much she could barely breathe.

But she had a job to do.

Plus, she was a person who didn't want anything permanent, so temporary relationships were good. Exactly what she had needed.

What she had with Jozef was exactly what she had wanted.

Until now. Now she had no idea what she wanted.

She went inside her dingy apartment, walked

back to the bathroom, stripped and let the water work its magic. After she calmed down, an unexpected thought struck her.

What if Jozef had changed his mind too?

His feelings for her were always right there in his eyes. She knew he more than cared deeply for her.

What if he was finally acknowledging that?

What if sending her the dress, inviting her personally to the gallery opening, was his way of making their relationship public?

He'd sent her a dress with an explicit card. He had to know there would be a possibility Geoffrey would open it—

And read the card.

A card that talked openly about their relationship.

Was this night about taking their relationship pubic?

They'd had a moment that morning, when they'd looked in each other's eyes and hated that she had to sneak out of the castle. Hated that no one, not even his family, could know what they were doing.

Maybe he'd had enough?

Still, his sons were going to the gallery opening. This couldn't be a date—

Except, his sons had begged off dinner after the gallery opening. They were thrilled to go to the gallery with their dad, part of the PR campaign to show the happy royals, but they also had their own lives.

Technically she and Jozef would be going out to dinner alone.

In public.

He had to know the press would make a big deal out of that.

She pulled her hair into a knot at the top of her head, then on whim decided to get fancy. She curled the strands that surrounded her face and dangled down her back and inserted some tiny flowers in strategic places.

She was about to get into her car to drive to the castle when she got a text saying a limo was outside her apartment.

He'd sent a limo.

Another thing he'd never done before.

Her suspicion that something important was happening grew, expanded into a big bubble of happiness in her chest.

For a guy who needed to keep his secrets, he was suddenly open as hell.

And he did nothing without thought, without purpose.

This meant something.

In her highest, sexiest shoes, she made her way down the stairs into the waiting limo.

The back seat was empty, but it wasn't even

a five-minute drive to the gallery. Still, it was enough time for her to realize that sending a limo pretty much meant he'd be escorting her home.

Like a date.

The realization that he might be making the most important move of their lives washed through her. But she'd already decided she wanted this. Wanted *him.* There was nothing more to it than that. She would have to step up. Face everything that dating him for real meant.

But she wanted him enough to change her entire life.

She entered through the back door of the gallery as the royals had and made her way to the front room where they stood chatting with the proprietor, a pretty, thirty-something woman, whose smile was so bright Rowan almost laughed. The star power of the three bachelor royals was enough to make any woman giddy.

The conversation stopped as she entered. The eyes of all three of the Sokol men widened.

Axel recovered first. "You look amazing!"

She walked over. "I'll bet you say that to all the girls."

But for the first time she realized that the dress Jozef had sent might be sexy and gorgeous, but there was also a certain sophistication to it. Definitely more classy than the purple dress with the slit up the side, this could be the gown of a queen.

The thought nearly paralyzed her. She was not imagining things. He really was inching them into the public eye together.

Jozef was thunderstruck by how beautiful she looked in the gown he'd chosen. But, of course, she was young. And playful and wonderful. He couldn't imagine her looking bad in anything.

He smiled at Axel and Liam all but falling over themselves to chat with her because he knew she'd be his that night.

He'd even arranged for them to have dinner in his private quarters so she could accompany him and not have to bow out at the restaurant because it was too public.

They stayed with the gallery owner for most of their hour. Then Fiona Barns gave them the last ten minutes to go back to whatever sections had piqued their interest. Axel and Liam went toward the sculpture exhibits.

Suddenly, he and Rowan were alone. Too tempted to resist, he drew her to him and kissed her and she melted in his arms. Anticipation stole through him. They could drive to the castle, have dinner and spend the rest of the night together.

At the end of their hour, they left the gallery

and walked to his limo, which was hidden in a back alley. But despite what Jozef considered tight security, a reporter had gotten through.

"Who are you with?" the guy called, holding up his phone, which was obviously in record mode.

When Jozef tensed, Rowan shook her head, the motion telling him to stand down. "This is my job, remember?"

He nodded.

"I'm Rowan Gray, I work for Sterling, Grant, Paris. King Jozef and I were just enjoying the gallery opening."

"Sterling, Grant, Paris? That's a PR firm, right?"

"Yes!" Jozef said, not waiting for her to answer. "Rowan has been helping Axel with the fall fundraiser. She's amazingly talented."

Rowan sneaked a peak at him. He resisted the urge to smile at her, knowing that any sort of gesture like that could be blown out of proportion.

He made a joke. "If you'll excuse us, we're sharing a cab."

The driver opened the door, Rowan slid inside and Jozef followed her. Once the driver was securely behind the wheel, with the soundproof glass between his section and the passenger section, Jozef laughed.

"That was fun!"

She glanced over with a frown. "Which part?"

"Okay. I liked the gallery. But I've never bantered with a reporter."

She winced. "That was your banter?"

He laughed. "I didn't say I was good at it. But I wanted to say, Rowan and I are going back to the castle to make passionate love and eat dinner. And I didn't. I shifted the conversation to you and how good you are at what you do. You know, so when you begin your own firm people will remember you."

She stared at him, and he could see in her eyes that he'd said or done something that confused her.

Finally, she said, "We're eating dinner at the castle?"

Of all the things he'd said, he'd genuinely believed that was the least offensive, but obviously it was the one that bothered her most.

"My parents left at noon. Both the boys bailed on me. Meaning, I don't have to go to the restaurant. We can go back to my quarters and be alone."

She studied him for a few minutes, then said, "You didn't want to go to the restaurant with *me*?"

"We could have. You are my PR person." He shifted on his seat, uncomfortable, but not because of her questions. It was her seriousness that sent prickles up his spine. "We have a legitimate reason to be together." He paused. "I just wanted to be alone with you so we can be normal."

"You couldn't be normal in the restaurant?"

"I couldn't do this in the restaurant." He reached out and held her still so he could kiss her. "Or this." He ran his hands down the soft material of the sleeves of the gown. "Or this." With his hand at her nape, he deepened the kiss, awakening needs in himself that would have rendered him speechless if he hadn't already had all these feelings with her.

When he pulled back, she gazed into his eyes. "Why not? Why couldn't you do those things?"

He laughed. "Really? You know our situation."

"Yes. You're afraid of what people will think."

Her answer insulted him to his core. "I'm not *afraid* of what people will think! I'm more concerned about our privacy. You said it yourself last night. The press would be all over your past. It would be *you* who would be embarrassed."

"Yes. But the gossip and the embarrassment would die down."

He stared at her. "Really?"

"Eventually. It always does."

That confused him enough that he couldn't prevaricate. "What are you saying?"

"I'm not saying anything. But I thought things had changed between us."

The confusion that hit him was so stunning, he almost couldn't speak. "Between us? Yes. I think we feel more deeply for each other, but that doesn't change who I am or how I have to comport myself."

"Sure. I understand..." Her voice trailed off as she caught his gaze. "No. Actually, I don't. We laughed this morning as if we'd finally realized our situation didn't work. You sent me a gown and an explicit card that could have been opened by my assistant. You sent a limo for me—" Her eyes squeezed closed. "Oh, my God. I misinterpreted everything."

Numb for a few seconds, he said nothing, as he sifted through what she'd said to figure out what was going on. "You thought I'd changed my mind about our relationship being public?"

She searched his gaze and very carefully said, "Yes."

He wished he could. "My feelings are so strong for you that I wonder how I will survive when we have to part, but we both know we have to part. So why go through the drama of being seen together in public?"

She studied him again. Her serious eyes flickering enough that he knew she was thinking through something.

"Jozef, what would you say if I said I'm now wondering if we do have to part?"

His breath caught. Thoughts of waking beside her forever filled him with joy. But the reality of their life stopped them cold. She was the one who would suffer if they decided to continue their affair. Because one day it would come out. And when it did, she'd be inundated by the media.

"I'd say that you need to think carefully about what you're considering."

"Our feelings for each other are strong. We've spent enough time together to show me who you are and enough that you've seen my integrity, what I'm made of. I'm crazy about you. I thought you were crazy about me too."

He understood what she was saying because he'd thought the same things himself. Even as an urge to catch her and kiss her senseless raced through him, to agree with her and have a shot at keeping her in his life, his common sense prevailed.

He caught her hands, a silent entreaty that she should listen to what he was saying. "I *am* crazy about you. You are smart, funny, beautiful and so sexy I sometimes think I will never get enough of you."

"But you don't love me."

The need to disagree—to admit that the urgent longings that always raced through him when she was around had to be love—expanded in his chest.

But that was selfish. Oh, so selfish. No matter how much being with her allowed him to be his real self, to indulge his desires, to speak the truth, she didn't know what she was saying, the depth of trouble to which she'd open herself because she loved him.

She loved him.

His heart trembled, as the longing to accept her love roared through him.

But his life would bring her nothing but misery.

All his experience, all his breeding, poured through him like a rich, worthy wine. In that moment, he dropped his own yearnings and became a well-trained royal, who knew the realities of his life and wouldn't hurt her.

Refused to hurt her.

"Real love takes time. More time than we've spent together."

She shook her head. "I don't think so. I mean, sometimes, yes. But you and I had the thunderbolt. That flash of lightning that warned us early on that there was something special between us."

There was no way he could deny that, so he quietly said, "There is something special between us."

"But you don't think it's love."

Up to this point, he might have questioned it, but the feelings swamping him, the longings, the needs he knew would go unfulfilled for the rest of his life, told him otherwise.

Still, the ultimate love pushed him to do the right thing.

"No. I don't think it's love."

Rowan only stared at him. She couldn't understand how he didn't see what was right before him.

She shook her head. "If we don't at least explore the emotion of it, then what's been happening between us is just sex—"

She stopped as the truth of that rumbled through her. A reality so crystal clear that everything else she wanted to say drifted away to nothing.

He really didn't love her. He liked her. They were fun together—dynamite in bed. And from the guidelines *she'd* set, there had been nothing wrong with what they had.

She'd been the one to stupidly let her guard

down enough that she'd gotten real feelings for him that became love. She'd fallen hard enough, fast enough, that in the few hours of getting dressed that evening, she'd created a scenario that didn't exist. Seen things in his behavior that he hadn't meant.

Hell, she had been ready to give up her career—her *life*—for him.

Well, didn't she feel like a damned fool.

He softened his voice. "Rowan..."

She held up her hand. "Don't! There is nothing I hate worse than pity!" She leaned forward, tapped on the glass between them and the driver. "Stop here."

Jozef gaped at her. "What are you doing?"

"Spoiling your fun tonight, Your Majesty. Because while you were living in the moment, taking advantage of a really hot attraction, I was stupidly falling in love with you." When he tried to talk, she raised her hand a little higher. "I don't blame you. I set out the rules. I did not realize how charming you were or that I'd be willing to give up everything for you." She shook her head. "And I've got to tell you I feel more than a little stupid right now. So you not saying anything would work best for me."

The driver suddenly opened the back door. She attempted to slide out. He caught her hand.

"Please don't go. You're taking this all wrong."

She sniffed a laugh. "Actually, that's the first correct thing you've said all night. I did take this all wrong. What was happening between us. How we both thought about it. I got all that wrong. Good night, Your Majesty."

She exited and the driver quickly closed the door and returned to his seat behind the steering wheel before Jozef had fully processed what had happened. He nearly told the man to turn around, to take him to Rowan's apartment so they could fix this.

But that was the problem. They couldn't fix this.

She was younger than he was. *Too young for him.* He had sons closer to her age. She was also a career woman. His queen could not have a job outside the castle. And she was American. Outspoken. Independent.

All the things he liked about her were also things that would make her life miserable if she became his queen.

Her life would become a nightmare of vetting, gossip, constant questions from the press.

Marrying him would be far worse than her great humiliation.

Still, as his limo wove into traffic, all the feelings he'd had when she'd said she loved him poured through him. Joy and loss collided. He pictured waking up with her every morning, even as he pictured the press tearing apart her life.

And knew he'd made the right choice for *her.*

Not for himself. No. He'd miss her more than he could allow himself to ponder—

Because the hollow feelings he felt being driven to the castle door told him he would never forget her.

She was his one true love.

But he couldn't have her.

Though the gallery had only been a five-minute drive from Rowan's apartment, the walk back was much longer. At first, she raced toward her temporary home, but seeing that no one gave her a minute's concern, she slowed her pace. Eventually, she removed her high, high heels. Holding the skirt of her gown so she didn't get the hem dirty, she walked the remaining block to her apartment and then climbed the steps.

But she hadn't done a good job of protecting the soft white material from the dirty sidewalk. She'd have the gown cleaned, then return it to him.

Him.

The guy she loved who didn't love her.

Behind the closed door of her apartment, she took a long slow breath and closed her eyes. How had she let this happen?

Not just how had she let herself fall in love, but how had she fallen in love with a guy who didn't love her.

Again?

Tears pooled in her eyes and spilled over. She walked into her bedroom and fell face-first on the bed.

Oh, God. This hurt worse than her great humiliation. Because the source of *that* pain had been the embarrassment. This time, everything she felt was private. An ache of loss so deep and so pure she almost couldn't move.

She'd taken a chance, offered to give up everything for him and he'd politely refused.

A little voice whispered that she couldn't have been that wrong, couldn't have misread the signs that much. But he'd been very clear in his refusal.

He didn't want what she'd offered, and she had to face that. She needed cold, hard logic to constantly remind her that Jozef didn't love her. That even if what she felt was real, what he felt wasn't.

She stepped out of the pretty white gown, put on her pajamas and tried to sleep but couldn't.

She hadn't wanted to be a queen. She hadn't wanted to be royalty. But she loved Jozef and she would have sacrificed everything for him.

How could one man twist her emotions so much that she'd be willing to do that?

Because that's what he'd done. That's what he lived. And in her crazy love for him, she wanted to share his burden.

She had absolutely no idea how to live with this pain. Losing Cash had been embarrassing but losing Jozef *hurt.*

In a rare move, she took the weekend off to get her bearings. But when she tried to work on Monday morning, her brain was mush.

Geoffrey teased and cajoled, trying to get her to talk, but she shrugged him off. When Jozef called, she froze, staring at the phone.

Geoffrey quietly said, "Are you going to get that?"

"No."

"Okay, look. I know something happened on Friday night at the gallery. Maybe he's calling to fix it."

He wasn't calling to fix it because the only way to fix it would be to say he'd changed his mind. And he hadn't. He was a man who knew his mind. If he said he didn't love her, he didn't love her.

Which meant he was being a diplomat, calling to smooth things over. To soften the blow of admitting he didn't love her. She didn't need to hear it. She didn't want his pity.

"He can't fix it."

"Do you want me to answer just in case he has a business reason for calling?"

She shook her head no, but Geoffrey answered anyway.

"Good afternoon, Your Majesty… No, I'm sorry, Rowan's not here right now… Why do I have her phone? She forgot it." At that, Geoffrey caught her gaze and gave her an apologetic look. "Yes. I'll be sure to tell her you called."

As he hung up the phone, the walls closed in on Rowan. "I don't think I can stay here."

"Good. Let's go get coffee or something."

She paced her office. "No. I mean I can't stay here in Prosperita." She combed her fingers through her hair. "Geoffrey, I'm a cliché. I fell for the handsome King. Worse, a reporter saw us together Friday night. God knows if he's checking into my past."

She stopped as a million thoughts assaulted her, the biggest one being she did not give a flying fig if the media found her past and plastered it all over the front pages of every newspaper in the world. It had no bearing on who she was right now.

"You know what? My past sucked but I. Am. Over. It. What the hell am I doing here when my dad's having a birthday party next weekend?"

"I don't know. What the hell are you doing here? You haven't had a vacation in years. You should take one." Geoffrey laughed. "Want me to make airline reservations?"

"No. I can make them myself. And I'll call Pete and tell him I'm going home for my dad's party and to spend a few weeks visiting my family."

"Makes perfect sense to me."

She shook her head and Geoffrey rose to go into his office. The second he was out of her line of vision, she blew her breath out on a sigh. She was not being gutsy. She was emotionally exhausted. Her affair with Jozef had been the happiest time of her life and he'd rejected her. She'd been rejected by the most wonderful person she'd ever met.

Her eyes stung with tears again. She'd never get over him here in his country. She needed to go home.

CHAPTER FOURTEEN

JOZEF HUNG UP the phone and paced behind his desk.

Because he hadn't seen hide nor hair of her all weekend, he'd called to make sure she was okay. The fact that she wouldn't take his call didn't reassure him. He hated that he'd hurt her. But he genuinely believed this was for the best.

He'd thought about everything she'd said, and longing poured through him. He wanted everything she thought they could have. But she didn't know the real price of loving him—

Loving him.

Remembering that she'd said she loved him filled him with a yearning so intense he wanted to throw something against a wall. But he didn't.

He didn't.

He never did anything he wasn't allowed to do.

Maybe if he could tell her that, she would understand and not be so hurt?

He stopped pacing his office. She had a standing appointment with Axel every afternoon. He would simply be in Axel's office when she arrived. Then, hopefully, he could explain better, make her see this wasn't her problem, but his life.

He walked to Axel's office a few minutes before her scheduled time and when he ambled through the door, Axel rose.

"Dad?"

"Just thought I'd check in with you and Rowan. See how the fundraiser is doing."

"It's great," Axel said, stepping away from the chair behind the desk and offering it to his father. "You're going to love some of Rowan's ideas."

He took the seat of command. "I'm sure I will."

"Can I have Genevieve get us coffee?"

Jozef said, "No, I'm good," just as Pete Sterling entered Axel's office.

Pete stuttered to a stop. "Your Majesty."

Jozef rose. "Mr. Sterling. Did you enjoy my mother's birthday party the other night?"

Sterling all but glowed. "It was amazing. Rowan and I have been to various events like that, but never as guests. We're sort of background people."

Jozef held back a wince. That was how he knew Rowan didn't understand what she was suggesting. She might have been with him for weeks, but she saw his life through the eyes of an observer, not a participant.

"Speaking of Rowan," Pete said, setting his briefcase on the conference table in the corner of Axel's office before he opened it. "She's taking a vacation." He laughed. "Actually, she's on her way home right now." He pulled a few files from the briefcase. "Her mom is having a seventieth birthday party for her dad next weekend, so she's going to West Virginia."

Jozef blinked. The fact that his mom and her dad were close to the same age sort of floored him, even as he realized she was returning to a very small town where she would undoubtedly run into the guy who hurt her.

To top off all of that, she was getting away from him. Really away from him. He would never see her again.

"So," Pete said, laying packets of papers on Axel's desk. "This is her rundown of how we'll be promoting the event worldwide."

"Worldwide?" Jozef asked, picking up one of the packets.

Axel grinned. "I mentioned this, remember?

Rowan and I decided that with the proper promotion we could turn our festival into a yearly tourist attraction."

"Kind of like the running of the bulls," Pete said, looking up over his glasses at Jozef. "Without the bulls."

"And the running," Axel quipped. "This way we can centralize our tourism business. Give hotels and restaurants something to plug...and prepare for."

"Or something to steer travelers away from," Pete added. "Your hotels can say, we have crowds the first two weeks in October for our fall festival. If you want peace and serenity, come in the summer."

Jozef said, "Ah," as Pete and Axel beamed. He waited a beat before he asked, "And Rowan will be back to help finalize all this?"

"She asked for six weeks off. That takes us past your festival." Pete shrugged. "What can I say? She wanted time off."

Or she was preparing to leave Sterling, Grant, Paris and Pete didn't know—

Or she'd already left Sterling, Grant, Paris and Pete didn't want to mention that to a client?

Jozef couldn't ask. If she hadn't already quit, he didn't want to risk her plan to tell her current employer. If she had, what would he say? That he was glad for her?

He wasn't. Everything became confused. What they had wasn't supposed to end like this. Or this quickly. They were supposed to have until after the fall festival. Yet, she was gone. Now.

Always prepared for any contingency, he never found himself in a position of being surprised or left without a plan.

But she was gone.

And he was unprepared.

Forcing a smile, he picked up his packet of information about the festival and faced Axel. "I trust you. And from what I can see here, you are pointing us in a very good direction. I'm proud of you."

Taken aback, Axel said, "Thanks, Dad."

The expression on his son's face sent more confusion through Jozef. His son appeared genuinely surprised by the compliment.

Pete all but bowed as he left the room, and though Jozef was accustomed to people respecting his position, everything about it felt out of sync today.

He returned to his office and tried to leaf through the packet of information Axel and Rowan had put together, but his mind was all over the place. He sat staring out the window, watching as the afternoon sun dipped.

Everything was so damned quiet.

He tried to remember the sounds of his sons racing around the residence and couldn't. He tried to remember Annalise preparing for a holiday or a royal event and he couldn't.

But thoughts of Rowan walking around his home in one of his shirts made him smile. Thinking about borrowing the vehicles of his drivers caused him to laugh out loud. Sneaking to her apartment. Talking about everything and nothing. Those were etched in his brain. Those made him laugh even as they tightened his chest.

He'd finally gotten a taste of romantic love and the joy of it.

He could not believe he would never see the object of that love again, but, worse, he knew all these wonderful memories he had of her would fade with time.

It would be as if he hadn't even known her.

The love of his life and he would forget her in the morass of ruling his country.

Deep sorrow permeated his soul, something else he'd never known or felt. Losing her meant losing more than a person. A piece of himself also disappeared. A playful, happy guy he hadn't even known existed. A guy who'd been so wrapped up in his lover that being with her was his completion. He hadn't merely found his soul he'd found himself.

At eight o'clock his phone rang. Hoping it was Rowan, he grabbed it, but it was Liam. In the silence of his office, he felt himself being pulled back into the world he'd had before Rowan entered and sensed another piece of the guy she had helped him become flutter away.

In the days that followed, he tried to shift back into the life that had been granted to him by destiny, but he simply could not.

At the end of the week, Friday night, when his sons should have had dates, they'd made plans once again to watch a movie.

This time he knew they recognized that something was off. And just like Rowan, he didn't want anybody's pity.

He didn't bother to change after work, just walked directly to the small in-castle theater. Dressed in jeans and oversize T-shirts, his sons sat laughing at a cartoon they were watching as they waited for him.

Pain pierced his heart again. He had never been happier than when he was with Rowan. He had never been himself the way he could be with her. He'd believed that Annalise—the relationship he had with Annalise—was perfect because he never let his guard down but what he'd had with Rowan far exceeded that. He'd never wanted to be stiff and formal, even if stiff and formal had kept him in good standing with his parents, Castle Admin and the media.

His heart stumbled. He wanted to be the guy he was with her. He wanted that life. Tons of happiness. Maybe more kids. An adventure.

And lots of fodder for the press? Things to criticize?

The movie started and he lowered himself to one of the reclining chairs. But he couldn't stop thinking about his life, about how different he had been with Rowan… About how happy he had been with Rowan.

Truth overshadowed his thoughts, though. He couldn't put Rowan through what would happen if they brought their relationship out in the open and ultimately married—

Could he?

No. He could not. That was why he wasn't with her now.

He glanced at Liam. He loved his sons in the most protective, parental way possible, yet he would be putting Liam through it.

The weight of his job pushed down on his shoulders and the sense that he had had enough filled him. It suddenly seemed all wrong.

He was the King. And though every citizen of his island had the right to hold him accountable for his decisions, no one had the right to monitor his private life, to criticize his choices, to hold his sons to the kinds of standards that would crush an ordinary man.

And *that's* what needed to change. Not him. Not Liam. And certainly not Rowan.

The way Castle Admin let the press rule them was the problem. He'd flirted with the idea of firing Art Andino…but what if he totally restructured Castle Admin?

The thought was so clear and so easy he couldn't speak for a minute as indescribable joy flooded him. He'd been trained to believe he had to be the person his position dictated—and he agreed to a point. He would never embarrass the Crown. But even the thought that there was another side to life, a wonderful, private, elevated side with Rowan, tempted him so much he couldn't let this stand. He had to change things.

He would change things.

And if he had to fight to change them, then he would fight…fight for *her.*

"Has either of you ever thought how you'd feel about me being in a relationship?"

Surprised, his sons glanced over at him.

Liam said, "You're not that old, Dad. You should want another relationship."

"I know, but if I get into another relationship, it will change things significantly around here."

Liam shrugged. "Axel and I are adults and very much on our own. It won't make any difference to us."

"I'm also thinking about changing how we handle the media."

Liam frowned. "The media?"

"Yes. I'm working on a plan that doesn't restrict their access but takes the teeth out of some of their criticisms. I might even have to restructure Castle Admin."

Axel laughed. "What?"

"I had this thought that if we stopped responding to media criticism and allowing Castle Admin to pander to them that they'd lose some of their power."

Axel thought about that, but Liam laughed. "I never thought of it that way, but we sort of do give them power by reacting when they point out what they perceive as flaws."

"I don't think it will be easy," Jozef said. "I think they'll fight back a bit, push us to get us to react, but I think if we stopped reacting and threatened to take away their access when they overstepped, we might be able to tame this tiger."

Liam said, "That would be great."

"You're just doing this to pave the way for your relationship," Axel said, then threw a handful of popcorn in his mouth.

Jozef said, “Maybe.”

“Oh, come on, Dad,” Axel said with a laugh. “You’re already in a relationship.”

Liam cast his father a confused look. “You are?”

Axel laughed. “You didn’t see a change in him the past few weeks?” When Liam still looked confused, Axel sighed. “When he was with the PR lady? Rowan?”

Liam grinned. “Seriously, Dad? She is…”

“She’s hot is what she is,” Axel said. “And incredibly smart.”

Jozef squeezed his eyes shut. He didn’t know whether to be embarrassed or to scold his sons for talking about him as if he weren’t in the room.

“So,” Axel said. “Are you going to go after her?”

“After her?” Liam frowned again. “Did she leave?”

Axel snorted. “Liam, you have to keep up or when you’re King, Castle Admin will walk all over you.” He glanced at his dad. “Of course, if we dismantle Castle Admin, they won’t be walking over any of us.”

Jozef rose. “That’s the plan.” He turned to Liam. “You have lots of time to learn to be observant.” He faced Axel. “And you only picked up on something between me and Rowan because you worked with her."

He headed to the door. "And I *am* going after her."

After over a week in Manhattan to look at potential sites for the offices for her new PR firm, Rowan made it to West Virginia. She'd needed some time working on her plan and new life, to get herself past the misery of losing Jozef. Her heart still hurt, but she was feeling more like herself. Enough that she could finally go home. She piled her suitcase, purse and carry-on into a rental car and drove the winding mountain roads to Convenience. Nestled in a rich, green forest, the little town hadn't changed in eight years.

She pulled her rental into the driveway of her parents' redbrick ranch house, with attached two-car garage. Yellow mums and pale pink hydrangeas bloomed in flower beds beneath the big windows on either side of the front door.

The garage door suddenly opened. Her mom raced out. A short woman whose red hair had begun to darken, she was the picture of happiness.

"Rowan! Oh, my God! You're *here*!"

She squeezed her daughter so tightly that

Rowan dropped her carry-on bag and laughed. "You just saw me this spring."

Her mom pulled back, studied her face. "I know. But you're here! You're home!"

Rowan whispered. "For a very special event."

Her mom motioned for her to lower her voice even more. "He still doesn't know about the party."

"And he's also losing his hearing," Rowan reminded her mom with a laugh. "He won't hear us if we whisper."

"Whisper what?" her dad, said, strolling out of the garage. He caught Rowan in a big hug, then kissed her cheek before he released her. "I see you're back."

"For about a week," Rowan said, keeping her voice light and cheerful, as she glanced around, waiting for the emotion of her great humiliation to overtake her, but none came.

Instead, she saw the quiet street of her hometown, rows of various types of houses from Cape Cod and Craftsmen styles to ranch houses and Colonials. Some were brick, some were painted various colors, but all the yards were neat as a pin and decorated with flower gardens.

But as much as she loved this town, her parents, this house, it wasn't home anymore. A horrible sense of loneliness overtook her. Not because she missed Paris. Because she missed Jozef.

She immediately wondered what he would think of her home, her town. She tried to shove that thought out of her head, but it wouldn't leave. She wanted him to see her town, to know her, because she wanted him to love her. Leaving Prosperita had been the most difficult thing she had done because she'd known she would never see him again. He wouldn't seek her out. He *couldn't* seek her out. And she had no reason to return to his country.

What they had, those wonderful couple of weeks, was all she would get. Though she tried to be happy for having known him, the ache in her heart radiated to her entire body. She'd thought she'd loved Cash, but what she felt for Jozef made that pale in comparison.

And now she no longer had a great humiliation, she had a real broken heart.

"Come inside," her dad said, looping his meaty arm over her shoulders. "We'll get a beer."

A beer.

It had been a while since she'd had a beer. But she was home. Funny, that she had run from this town because of a broken relationship and now the only place she believed she could fix this broken heart was here. With her family.

Her sister and brother were happy to see her. Both had gotten engaged. Both insisted she had to come to their weddings. Her heart sank again. Here she was thirty, and she'd managed to fall in love with the one man who couldn't love her. While her younger siblings raced past her in making their lives, she had stagnated.

The thought flummoxed her. In the eight years since her great humiliation, she'd believed marriage was a full stop, not a part of making a life. Odd how she didn't feel that way anymore. She finally saw love and marriage was just the beginning.

She took her dad to the diner for dinner when her mom pretended to have a headache and not be able to cook. He'd frowned, but when Rowan acted thrilled to be going to the diner for their famous chili, he relented.

Most of the people they'd run into didn't even mention Cash, and if her heart weren't so broken over losing Jozef that might have made her laugh. By the time they returned to the redbrick ranch, she was exhausted from pretending to be happy.

They walked up to the driveway and her dad put his hand on her forearm to stop her.

"What's the matter, kitten? You're not yourself."

They were supposed to enter through the garage so her mom could pop on the lights, and everybody could jump up and yell surprise. This was not the time to pour her heart out to her dad. Though she longed to throw herself into his big arms and weep, have him comfort her as she cried it all out, she couldn't.

"Nothing. I'm fine."

"Oh, come on. You can't kid a kidder."

She laughed. "You always say that, but I pulled the wool over your eyes a lot when I was a kid."

He batted a hand. "I just let you think that."

"You did?"

"Yeah. A kid's gotta have some fun. I let you think you got away with things." He pointed at the garage door. "Just like I let your mom believe I hadn't figured out about the surprise party."

She sighed. "If I don't get you in that garage soon, Mom's gonna think I screwed up."

"Well, we can't have that."

"No, we can't," she agreed, catching his arm and dragging him to the garage door. She hit the button on the remote door opener her mom had given her and the two doors rose simultaneously. The lights flashed on. The fifty people in the garage jumped up and yelled, "Surprise!"

Her mom raced out and hugged her dad. Over her mom's shoulder, he winked at Rowan.

Then he turned to face the crowd with a smile. "Hey! Thanks!" He walked in and began shaking the hands of the guests standing around the two long tables filled with food. "Nice to see you. Thanks for coming. Nice to see you."

Twenty minutes later, he sat beside her on a bench along the back wall. "I turned seventy this week. It's a milestone. So it wasn't a stretch to guess your mom was planning something. If you want to surprise someone you need to have better timing."

She bumped his shoulder with her own. "Right."

She took a long breath, taking in the cooling September air.

"You're not going to tell me what's wrong?"

"Nope."

"You can't always hide from your troubles, kitten. You have to talk to someone sometime."

"I can't, Dad. I had all these wonderful plans of starting my own PR firm, then I fell in love, and nothing seems to have any meaning anymore."

"Whoa! Whoa! You fell in love?"

"With someone who doesn't love me." There. She'd said it. Her heart shredded again with the pain of loss and ridiculous longing.

"Well, he's an idiot."

"No. He's a king."

Her dad gaped at her. "What?"

"A king." She opened her arms, motioning around the garage. "And I'm about as common as they come. But there's more to it than that. Duty and responsibility. A need to have his life planned to a tee. I don't fit."

It hurt to say that too.

And she was at the end of her ability to talk about Jozef. She rose from the old bench. "You know what? I'm kind of tired. I think I'll go inside and get a shower. If the party's still going on I'll come out and say good-night."

"Honey, I don't think you should..." Her dad's face scrunched in confusion then he rose and pointed down the street. "What is that?"

She followed the direction of his pointing finger and saw a long black limo pulling up in front of her house. Her heart stopped.

The driver emerged, walked to the back of the limo and opened the door.

Jozef stepped out.

Rowan stood frozen. Her eyes wide.

He ambled up the sidewalk and to the driveway, toward the open garage doors.

Standing over her shoulder, her dad leaned down and said, "Now, that's how you do a surprise."

She would have laughed but her mouth wouldn't move. She couldn't breathe. Confused silence filled the garage.

Wearing the red and blue polo shirt she'd bought him for the soccer game, he entered the garage and walked up to her. "I'm sorry."

Knowing the eyes of all fifty people were on her, because the King of an entire country was in her family's *garage,* she couldn't process what he was saying. "What?"

"I came to some conclusions in the weeks after you left." His gaze held hers. "I do love you. I didn't want to say it the other day because I didn't want you to go through the media circus that would follow if we began dating."

"Oh. Okay."

He laughed. "I get the sense I surprised you so much you're speechless, and I'm not sure you're fully understanding me when what I have to say is really important."

She shook her head, forcing herself not to look at the fifty people who were staring at them and keeping her attention on Jozef.

"I talked with my sons. We're all tired of the media bullying us. We're all on board with accountability. But we really do not believe they should have any say in our private lives."

"No matter what you do, they'll push back."

"Let them. We've decided that if we don't react to the less important things, they will lose their hold on us."

She considered that. It was advice she'd given to a client a time or two. She finally understood what was going on. He was here for advice.

She raised her chin, refusing to let any of the pain she felt seep through. After all, he saw her more as PR person and a friend than his lover. She'd answer his few questions and he'd leave.

"It could work, but at some point, once they realize what you're doing, they are going to push back. You'll have an uphill battle for a few years."

He held out his hand. "Want to fight it with me?"

The pain turned to ice. "You're here to hire me?"

"No. I'm here to ask you out on a date. A real date."

"So you can attack your media head-on?"

"No. Hopefully so that you'll remember you love me and eventually we'd get married." He rifled in his pocket. "I have a ring. I love you enough to face the gates of hell to keep you in my life. When I told you no it was because I didn't want to see you hurt. But you're a tough cookie. What we had is worth fighting for."

She stared at him. His handsome face. His once brooding eyes that sparkled with amusement.

"You love me?"

"I do."

Her dad came strolling out. "Hey. Hey. Save the 'I do's' for the wedding." He held out his hand. "I'm Rowan's dad."

Then her mom eased out and introduced herself. "I'm her mom."

Her sister came out. "Younger sister."

"I'm Fontain. Brother."

Everyone shook hands with Jozef and he handled it all with grace and dignity. He explained who he was and where he was from and all fifty people nodded as their eyes widened.

He ate a ham sandwich and drank two beers with her dad while answering a hundred questions. Then when interest in him died down. Rowan and Jozef sat on the front porch swing.

"I can't believe you're here."

Jozef glanced around. "I can't believe I'm here either." He slid his arm along the back of the swing. "But you know what? You make me want a life, a real life."

She cuddled closer, glancing down at her

ring that sparkled in the porch light. "Doesn't get much more real than this."

He laughed. "I don't think you understand what a gift it is to be able to be yourself."

"I think I do now." A thought hit her and she gasped. "Where's your security?"

"Discreetly hidden." He took a breath. "Actually, when we made our plan, they told me that you can't sleep at your parents' house tonight. The detail they brought doesn't have enough men to keep guard over a house and a hotel. You have to come back to the hotel with me."

"Did you just make that up to get me to come back to your hotel and sleep with you?"

He laughed. "No. I swear. This is about security. But it does work in our favor."

She smiled at him. "Yeah. It does."

They stayed at the party another hour, then she packed a bag and they left for the hotel. They'd be back to say goodbye to her parents the next day, but she knew she was embarking on the greatest adventure of her life.

Not marrying a king—

Being married to a guy who loved her enough to change *his* world for her.

It was going to take a lot of kisses to thank him for that.

EPILOGUE

AXEL STOOD AT the altar of Prosperita's cathedral. In full dress uniform, he, his brother, Liam, and his father looked about as official as a king and two princes could be.

Rowan Gray walked down the aisle toward them on the arm of her father. Through two years of his daughter dating the King, Rowan's dad had become accustomed to all things royal and he looked as calm and comfortable as he did in the backyard of his West Virginia home.

Axel took great pride in that. He'd not only realized his father was falling for the lovely PR person sent to set him up on dates, he'd also taken the lead when they made visits to her family's home. He was damned good at pool—as good as her father and brother—and he could now grill a mean hamburger. Not that he needed to here in Prosperita, but he prided himself on being the bridge of the family. The one who could create a way for groups to get along.

He should be in the diplomatic corps for the country. Now that his work with making the fall festival a tourist attraction was taking off like a rocket, maybe someday he would.

Rowan arrived at the altar. The sparkles of her flowing gown and veil were totally outdone by the sparkles in her eyes. Good God, she loved his dad.

Which was amazing and touching. He loved his dad too, and after seven years without Axel and Liam's mom, Jozef Sokol deserved the happiness Rowan had brought into his life. Axel loved her for that. Loved her for bringing life back to the castle. Loved her for being no one's pushover.

In fact, if he were honest, he'd have to admit he'd had a bit of a crush on her himself, if only because she'd never let Castle Admin push her around. And with her PR background the press was putty in her hands.

He laughed, then covered it with a cough in the solemn confines of the cathedral.

He took a breath and turned when his father and Liam did, letting the wedding service ebb and flow around him. He didn't like the public side of their lives. He much preferred being the bridge between the royals and whoever they were bringing into their inner circle, intentionally or not.

But he could endure the pomp and circumstance.

A motion at the back of the church caught his attention and he scowled. Damn it all anyway! The new security employee was flapping her arms about something.

The woman had no idea of decorum.

He had no problem with women serving in their security details, but he did not believe this one had been properly vetted.

Maybe this was one of those times when he should interfere? His dad had been busy. Liam was always being observed so he couldn't stick his nose somewhere that it didn't belong, but Axel could.

If there wasn't a very, very good reason for whatever she was flapping her arms about, she would be fired.

The ceremony ended. His father and Rowan walked out of the church, under the arch of swords and raced to the limo.

He and Rowan's sister, a bridesmaid, and Liam and one of Rowan's friends from Paris, another bridesmaid, walked out of the church and he forgot all about the security person.

The sun was warm, the entire country was celebrating the long-awaited wedding and Axel was so happy for his dad he could have burst.

* * * * *

If you enjoyed this story,
check out these other great reads from
Susan Meier